WORM FIDDLING NOCTURNE
IN THE KEY OF A
BROKEN HEART

STORIES

WITHDRAWN

WORM FIDDLING NOCTURNE IN THE KEY OF A BROKEN HEART

KIMBERLY LOJEWSKI

BURROW PRESS | ORLANDO, FL

This publication is made possible in part by our Founding Sponsors:

Burrow Press thrives on the direct support of its subscribers, and generous support from grants, companies, foundations, and individuals.

Published by Burrow Press
PO Box 533709
Orlando, FL 32853
burrowpress.com

ISBN: 978-1-941681-71-8
LCCN: 2018935967

Book Design: Ryan Rivas
Cover Art: Jerome Robbins Dance Division, The New York Public Library.
"The fairy grotto" The New York Public Library Digital Collections. 1867.

To my mother
for always listening to my stories

CONTENTS

WORM FIDDLING NOCTURNE IN THE KEY OF A BROKEN HEART

It isn't just a pastime. It's an art. An outsider might wonder just why worm fiddling is such a big deal around here, but that's what makes them an outsider. If you grew up in Break-A-Leg, you would know that not only is it the quickest route to local celebrity, it also keeps your family fed and fat as hogs. My uncle Josiah has been practicing at it for over thirty years.

Uncle Josiah has a twin brother named Obediah. They live on opposite sides of an invisible boundary in the swamps. Josiah wakes up before the sun, wearing stained overalls and galoshes, bucket handles splayed in his fingertips, cutting a proud silhouette against the dawn. Obediah sleeps until noon. Uncle Obie wanders around Castle Chinkapin in a velveteen cape he found at a thrift store. He likes to lounge out by the alligator moat, leaf through books on architecture and design, and pop his glass eye in and out when he's thinking hard about something.

Uncle Obie loves to take trash and turn it into something useful. Castle Chinkapin, for instance, is made entirely of garbage. The base structure comes from the discarded tin plates of a printing press, giving the castle a scaly, metallic look despite its turrets and towers. He built the castle from the ground up before I was born. In its infancy, it was a tin casing, empty on the inside and reflecting back the summer sun so fiercely that low-flying planes would often point it out as they passed. Now it's decorated with ribbons and banners, stained glass mirrors, hot air balloon mobiles, statues made from bicycle wheels and beer cans, roses growing out of old boots and rubber tires, a clothes-hanger-animal menagerie, and outdoor art installations like the broken mirror maze and the glow-in-the-dark painted garden.

Uncle Josiah considers Castle Chinkapin an eyesore and an embarrassment. He's never forgiven Uncle Obie for abandoning the family tradition to build his trash palace. We're a worm-grunting family. That's what Josiah says. He's held the championship title for the past ten years. Before that his daddy, my grandpa, was the official Worm Fiddling King. It runs in our blood. Uncle Josiah says to be a Pierce is to be a born and bred worm charmer.

Sometimes I feel torn between the two of them. I like Uncle Obediah's sense of disheveled artistic whimsy. And I'm impressed by Uncle Josiah's dedication to craft and skill. Here in Break-A-Leg they are local celebrities. This puts a lot of pressure on me to choose a legacy and carry it on. My uncles have raised me ever since my mother ran away from Break-A-Leg and left me behind.

•

My best friend is an alligator wrestler named Sweets. That's his nickname, of course. His real name is Stanley Sweets. His mother also left Break-A-Leg when he was just a boy, and his father disappeared into the swamps one day and was never found. That happens from time to time, especially in the alligator wrestling business. Sweets lives with his gran a few trailers down from Josiah. We've grown up alongside each other.

Sweets loves listening to my uncles bicker and brag. One time, I overheard Gran Sweets saying they were like fathers to him. He goes to every worm charming competition that Uncle Josiah competes in, and he's helped Uncle Obie with a lot of the handiwork around Castle Chinkapin. Sweets was the one who found the old shrimping trawler way out where the swamps meet the sea. He helped Obediah convert it into the Boat in the Moat Café. Now it serves as a snack bar for hungry tourists.

"Lemon!" Uncle Obie calls. "Where's my coffee?"

I pour two cups and hurry back to where he's stretched out on his recliner like swamp royalty. Under his cape he has on swimming trunks that are a few sizes too big for his skinny frame. The sound of the cicadas rises up around us in the warm morning. The alligators floating in the moat watch us with dull eyes as we sip coffee in silence.

I'm sweating already. Break-A-Leg is like a steaming pot of black waters, bullfrogs, mosquitoes, Spanish moss, and wet earth. And worms. I peer across the moat looking for Sweets' old pickup truck. We're going to be late for school again.

"I've been thinking," Obie says. "It's about time you went to work. What would you say to a full time job in the Café?"

Sometimes Uncle Obie lives so much in his fantasy world that he forgets about reality. "I have school," I say.

"We're talking careers here, kid. I'm offering you the chance to be a princess."

I tread carefully. "I don't think I'm ready for the responsibility," I tell him, scratching at a bug bite on my knee. "That's serious business."

Uncle Obie nods. He seems to accept that. "Maybe in another year or so then. If someone else doesn't snap up your position."

"Maybe."

"Don't tell me you're getting involved in all that worm nonsense." He pops out his glass eye and rolls it around in his palm.

The best way to handle this is always to change the subject. "There's a Break-A-Leg pig roast on Sunday," I tell him. "The high school is raising money for the library."

"Books are important," says Uncle Obie. I sense he's about to make one of his grand gestures. "I'll donate a pig. Or an art piece."

I'm relieved to see the sun gleaming off of Sweets' truck as it rounds the corner. "Sorry, Lemon!" he says, pulling up beside us. "Hi, Obediah. Nice day out."

Obediah holds up his coffee cup in a cheers. "Feels like a devil's fart." I wave goodbye, climb into the truck beside Sweets, and we tear off through the pumpkin-colored dust.

"We're going to be late."

Sweets nods and grins apologetically. He has the tanned skin and strong features of the Seminole Indians on his gran's side. His eyes are the color of muddy water in the sunlight. I resigned myself to being in love with him a long time ago.

I notice one of his arms is freshly bandaged. "The Swamp Ghost?" I ask, lifting an eyebrow.

"She's getting big," Sweets says. "And strong."

Ten summers ago, Uncle Josiah found a creamy-skinned, blue-eyed alligator hatchling and gave it to me and Sweets to raise. White alligators are really rare. This is the first one we've had around these parts in several generations. She's not an albino, but a real leucistic white gator, a genetic anomaly, stronger and swifter than her pink-eyed doppelgangers. The

Seminoles call them Swamp Ghosts. Some people think they are magic. Some people think they're bad omens. Sweets thinks this gator is the ticket to making it big in alligator wrestling. He spends all of his time with her, to the point where he's been neglecting all the other gators he's trained over the years.

"It's just a nick," he says, seeing my look. "She barely grazed me."

I have a completely rational fear that Sweets is going to end up in a gator hole of his own making. He's got no objectivity anymore. It's like he's forgotten that the Swamp Ghost isn't just a mysterious and mythical piece of folklore, she's an aggressive apex predator. If she doesn't get to him, it's only a matter of time before one of the hundreds of bellowing male gators trying to court her does. You can hear the racket all the way from Uncle Josiah's trailer. It's like the jaws of hell have opened up. Entire congregations of suitors, hulking and sinewy, pine with frustration for her precious moon-white osteoderms.

I'm so caught up in gloomy scenarios I almost don't notice the letter stuck under the ratty old windshield wipers of the pickup. Sweets sees me notice and grabs it first. I try to tear it out of his hands, but he stuffs it down the side of his seat before I can get to it. A love letter, no doubt. Girls love him. More so because he doesn't seem to notice or care. He's much more interested in his alligators.

"Come on, Lemon," Sweets says when he notices my sulky expression. "I don't ask you about the boys hanging around your locker or trying to walk you to class. What are you so worried about? Nothing is ever going to change us."

This is part of what I'm worried about.

"Come have dinner at Gran's tonight," he says. "She'd love to see you. Bring Josiah."

I nod.

We don't get in trouble for being late to school. Sweets is good at dazzling the teachers. He hates school, preferring to spend his time outdoors, but I always feel relieved when I step in the front doors of Break-A-Leg High. The swamp seems to recede some beneath the weight of learning. School is my way out of here. I want options for myself that don't include trash castles or charming worms.

•

The outside of Uncle Josiah's trailer is filled with huge tubs of worms that shimmer and stink in the sun. The worms boil around in quivering masses of tangled annuli. Thousands of them burrowing in and out of each other helplessly.

"You're just in time to help me sort," Josiah says. "I caught some big ones. Must be close to a foot. Something in the soil these days."

I've been helping him for so long that I know exactly how much a handful of worms weighs. Sometimes I check myself with the scale for the satisfaction of it, but I never need it. This makes Josiah proud. He says it's proof I've got worm-fiddling blood.

"How's that crazy brother of mine?" he asks.

"He had his glass eye out when I left," I say. "But he's offered to donate a pig to the school barbecue."

I know Josiah is thinking he'll donate two pigs.

"He been getting visitors out there?"

I nod. No one was more surprised than me when tourists actually began visiting Castle Chinkapin. Uncle Obie charges a lofty ten dollars for admission. To Uncle Josiah, ten dollars equals about twenty packaged containers of worms, and the appeal of a coat-hanger menagerie is completely lost on him.

I try to distract him. "Do you know Aristotle called earthworms the intestines of the earth?"

Josiah grins. His gappy smile is gentle and proud. "Smart man," he says. "And you're a smart girl, Lemon. You shouldn't spend so much time over at Obediah's. How about you come fiddling with me tomorrow morning? The contest is coming up soon. You need your practice if you're going to take the title this time."

I nod. We finish the worm sorting and Josiah heads off to make his deliveries while I start my homework. My mind wanders as I try to study. The bellows of the alligators and trickles of sweat on my body are distracting me. I turn the little rotating fan on high but it only seems to circulate the heat. I get up and prowl the length of the trailer, my skin goose-fleshing at the deep bass rumbles coming from the Sweets property. Alligators use infrasound when they call for their mates. It's a frequency similar to a tuba or a pipe organ. When they really get to roaring it feels just like the ground is rattling.

I drink a can of Coke out of the fridge and feel a little better. I go outside where the sun is finally relenting and see a few straggler worms wriggling about the dusty driveway. Few things kill earthworms aside from a good drying out, so I pick them up carefully and walk down to the edge of the swamps to set them down where the soil is moist. "You're the lucky ones," I tell them as they burrow sightlessly into the warm belly of the earth. "You're going to get out of here."

With the sun filtering down through the swoops of Spanish moss that drape the graceful cypress trees, and the dark mysterious shine of the water, the swamp looks suddenly beautiful and golden. The water lilies are turned towards the last rays of the sun. The smaller, spindly never-wets are beginning to bloom in yellow clusters above the opaque surface of the water. Everywhere I see things living and breathing. Moving. In the soil, on the trees, under the water. It's almost overwhelming.

That night, over the roaring of the alligators, Uncle Josiah and Gran Sweets discuss the size of this spring's worms. She's made fry bread and a cabbage salad from her own garden.

"Even the cabbages are large," she says, as if to prove a point.

Sweets and I look at each other and roll our eyes. I wonder if we'll have conversations like this one day. I try to listen to their mind-numbing talk. Cabbages and worms. If there are any hidden meanings, they are well encrypted.

"When are you going to make it official and enter your Swamp Ghost in a real wrestling contest?" Josiah asks, the conversation finally turning our way.

Sweets' eyes light up and I suffer a jealous pang. They have never lit up that way for me. "She's ready," he brags. "She's already past the weight qualifications by a mile. She's bigger and stronger than any other alligator her age." He sounds the way dopey parents do when they think their kid is the smartest thing in the world.

"Christ's sake," I say. "That's only because they mature more quickly in captivity."

We all know this already. The Sweets family has been raising alligators for generations. I just want them to realize that the Swamp Ghost is not so special. Neither are the worms this year. Or the cabbages. Break-A-Leg is the same predictable place it's always been.

"Language, Lemon," Josiah scolds.

Sweets looks genuinely hurt.

"A real Swamp Ghost only comes along once in a few generations," Gran Sweets says softly. "They are gifts from the spirit world. To stare one in the eye is good luck. To wrestle one is to become a man above all men."

I use the only defense I have against Seminole folklore. "She's just like any other leucistic animal," I say. "She has reduced pigmentation from a recessive gene. Other than that she's nothing but a plain old bad-tempered adolescent female gator."

Gran Sweets gives me a look that lets me know the Swamp Ghost isn't the only bad-tempered female around. Usually I like her stories and superstitions. I guess the heat has gotten to me today.

"Come on," Sweets says, clearing the empty plates and starting the coffee maker. "I'll take you out to see her. She's really something in the moonlight."

Outside the sky is clear and star-filled, but the air is hot and heavy. I imagine our bodies leaving imprints on the night. The guttural croaking and bellowing of male alligators is deafening. They surround the reinforced pen, climbing on top of one another to press their snouts against the layers of heavy wire. Sweets has built a little platform outside the back of the trailer that is high enough for us to stand on and keep clear of snapping jaws and thrashing tails. It shudders to the beat of their heartsick serenades. All alligators bellow in B flat, the musical essence of reptilian lovemaking.

"You're pissing off Gran," Sweets says. "You know she hates it when you talk like a scientist."

I see the gleaming white ridges of the Swamp Ghost's broad back. She is basking in the moonlight, wallowing in the chorus of grunts and roars. She's much bigger than the last time I saw her. Her tail is fat and glorious and gleaming beneath the stars. A tail made to initiate death rolls and propel her impressive mass fearlessly through dark waters. She turns her head to the side and regards me with cold-blooded malice.

"She's creepy," I tell him. "And she wants to mate. Why don't you just let her go?"

Sweets stares at me as if I have lost half my brain. "Because I need her. You know that. I can make my name wrestling a Swamp Ghost. It will make Gran proud."

I look at Sweets and try to think of a reason to touch his face. He's staring off toward his alligator with a dreamy expression. I smack a mosquito on his cheek.

The Swamp Ghost is watching. She opens her jaws in a clear act of menace. The bugs are swarming us and the croaks and snarls of the alligators surrounding the pen are too much for me.

"I've got to go," I say. "I'll see you tomorrow morning."

I leave without Uncle Josiah. Sweets stands on the porch and watches me disappear into the darkness. I don't stumble on the way home. I know every cypress knee, muddy bog, and twisted tree root of this swamp. When I get back to Josiah's trailer I find a note from Obediah on the door that reads:

Brother,

I need Lemon this weekend. I'm working on a top-secret project. It will be the most magnificent art installation that Break-A-Leg has ever seen.

King O

·

In the morning, me and Josiah set out with our buckets before dawn. Wearing overalls and galoshes, we trudge deep into the thickest part of the swamps, where the ground is rubbery and thick with moss. I have my own set of fiddling sticks, consisting of a wooden stob and a flat rooping iron. They aren't quite as large and unwieldy as Josiah's but they do the trick. I chose the wood, hammered the metal, and carved the notches in them myself. Every Pierce, with the exception of Obediah, has his own worm charming technique and equipment.

We set to work in large patches far enough away from each other to maximize our efforts. By the time I've got my stob pounded into the ground, my ponytail is sticking to the back of my neck and my shirt is soaked through. Worm fiddling is hot work. I begin the slow, steady sawing motions, rubbing the rooping iron back and forth against it, creating a tempo that sets the swamps humming. Uncle Josiah is more of a grunter. He uses a metal plane for his stob and releases low-groaning staccato vibrations into the earth—the bass to my soprano.

All at once, the swamp is alive with shivering earthen melodies and the ground around us erupts with worms. Glistening, roiling masses of worms, like the earth is spewing up its insides. They wriggle toward the surface, turning up mud and soil in their desperation. A trained fiddler can imitate the underground vibrations of voles, moles, and even digging armadillos, causing the worms to flee the safety of the earth as fast as they can until they are exposed and squiggling in the sunlight. They break out of the soil in a panic-stricken blind quiver. They think they're escaping an underground symphony of predators.

We work in a practiced rhythm. When Josiah and I work like this together it feels like a habit as old as time. We never talk. We move in unison. Once there's a thick layer of worms covering the ground, we pause to scoop them into buckets, then continue on with our work. Every so often Uncle Josiah looks over at me proudly. I know what he's thinking. He's thinking we've got this year's worm fiddling title in the bag.

I fill my buckets quickly. I even beat Josiah.

"You'll take the title this year, Lemon," he says. He's covered in dirt and slime but he looks happy. "You're going to be Queen of the Worm Fiddling Festival."

But I don't want to be the Worm Fiddling Queen. It surprises me to realize this. The sun is out and tendrils of mist and moisture steam up from the ground to burn off in the sky. "I need to get home and shower before school."

"I'm not worried at all," he says, as if I haven't spoken. "You're a Pierce. Worm charming is in your blood."

•

Sweets is quiet on the way to school. He has a new bandage, a big one on his shoulder. It's so fresh that a crimson bloom has stained his shirt. The Swamp Ghost is playing with him. The sight of it makes me feel sick, so I stare out the window blankly.

Today I skip lunch to read in the library. The biggest species of worm is found in Australia. The Giant Gippsland Earthworm can grow up to seven feet long. Its eggs are cork-sized and the worms are purple and blue. Aside from that they're just like Break-A-Leg's worms. Sightless. Thoughtless. Compelled by nature to spend their lives recycling earth. The book doesn't say whether or not you can charm a Giant Gippsland.

The day takes an unusual turn when Uncle Obediah arrives at school dressed in military finery and delivers a slaughtered pig for the weekend barbecue. He rolls the pig directly into the office using a wheelbarrow. A slippery trail of blood decorates the linoleum floor behind him.

"Lemon," he says, catching sight of me in the hallway. Students and teachers are staring. The hall's full of rubberneckers. "Did your uncle get my message? I need you to come to the castle after school today. I've got something big planned. Inspiration has *struck*!"

This causes as much buzz as the pig carcass. Everyone wants to know what Uncle Obediah has planned. In a town the size of Break-A-Leg, any news is big news. Of course Uncle Obie knows that. He thrives on all this attention.

"What do you think it will be?" Sweets asks on the ride home. There's another letter on his windshield, but I don't grab at it today. I feel a streak of irritation coming on. So far, what I've learned about love is that it consists mostly of mood swings and unpredictable emotions.

"Who knows?" I say.

As we pull into Uncle Obie's driveway, Sweets' tone gets serious. "Lemon, I need to tell you something." When we reach Castle Chinkapin, he parks the truck under an old oak tree and turns toward me. "I'm wrestling the Swamp Ghost at the Worm Fiddling Festival next week. Your uncle and Gran decided on it last night. It's about the only time Break-A-Leg gets any real publicity. And… she's ready."

My shock is dulled by the heat. "That is the stupidest thing I've ever heard, Sweets. You shouldn't even be play-tussling with her right now. She wants to mate. It's too dangerous."

The Swamp Ghost started out as *ours*. Both of ours. Before transforming into his own personal obsession. And she really *is* dangerous. She's been cooped up for a decade and denied all her natural she-gator instincts.

His defensiveness is immediate. "I don't think that's what's bothering you Lemon." He fiddles with his dressing and pauses a long moment before turning those muddy brown eyes my way. "I think you're worried I'll take the attention away from you winning the competition. I think you just aren't used to sharing the spotlight."

My mouth hangs open for a moment and then snaps shut. It's like I'm talking to a stranger. Sweets and I have been best friends since we were babies. We were abandoned together. We grew up together. I've loved him for nearly as long as that and a thousand times more than worms, championship titles, or being the heir to Castle Chinkapin. Loving Stanley Sweets is the one thing I'm sure I want to do in this world.

"Stanley Sweets." My voice quavers. I draw the words out carefully, calculating just how much I'm going to let him have it, but I chicken out and twist my anger into sarcasm. "Why would I care about sharing my worm-fiddling fame when I am already the princess of all this?" I gesture out to the beribboned mess of garbage around us. The trash castle in all its aluminum-turreted glory. The glow-in-the-dark painted garden, the alligator-filled moat, and the coat-hanger menagerie.

Uncle Obediah is passed out in a tin bathtub drunk as a lord, sunburnt and snoring, his cape pillowed beneath his head. A few scattered tourists peruse the grounds in bemused wonderment, taking pictures. A peacock struts past the truck and fans its tail at us.

Sweets is red-faced. He is just as unfamiliar with arguing as I am, but it seems like he needs to get something out. "You act like you're too good for this place, Lemon."

I take that like a smack in the face. We stare at each other for a moment before I get out of the truck and walk over to my uncle and shake him awake. Apparently the tourists have not paid admission, because the instant Obie's eyes snap open he leaps from the tub, his cape flapping behind him, and proceeds to hoot and chase the interlopers. "This is not a low-rent charity!" he yells, corralling them toward the ticket booth. I don't turn around to see Sweets leave.

It takes a while to restore order at Castle Chinkapin. Once Obediah has collected his dues and settled down, he unveils his plans to me. We are going to make an enormous paper-mâché rendering of the Swamp Ghost. Huge. Larger than life. Big enough to take up an entire room in the castle. Uncle Obie has designed a series of casts and molds, as well as collected an assortment of plaster and balloons to use for the project. I stare at the heap of odds and ends while he wanders off to charm some new visitors.

"They call me the Rembrandt of Refuse," I hear him say. "The da Vinci of Debris. The Wizard of Odds… and Ends!"

The Swamp Ghost. Of all the art projects he could have thought up. She is the literal representation of my problems with Sweets. My guts ache. I glare at his sketches and kick at the mold that is going to be her snout.

I don't cry much. I grew up with worms and alligators and men. Instead, I pick up rocks and hurl them at the tin-plate walls of Castle Chinkapin. With each dent my sadness turns into something tangible. Something solid. Uncle Obie watches me from the sidelines for a bit before joining in. He finds some rusted shovels for us to really bang up the aluminum with.

"Performance art," he says to the bewildered tourists as we smash away. They beeline back to their cars and speed off.

"Nice," Uncle Obie says, once we've exhausted ourselves. He gets his pipe and examines our handiwork. "Now it has texture. I believe I'll spackle some gems into these rivets."

•

The week before the Festival, Sweets stops picking me up for school and I have to borrow Uncle Obie's corn-fueled motorcycle. As if sputtering up to the curb smelling like greasy French fries isn't bad enough, on Wednesday, I see Stanley Sweets holding hands with one of the girls we used to dismiss as a pageant peacock. Tiffany-Ann, or Ann-Marie, or some other prissy double-barreled name like that. Big lamb eyes and curly blond hair. Just the kind of girl he used to think was ridiculous.

•

The day of the festival, it's like the swamp is in agreement with my mood. We get an early summer storm that boils up in the sky and hangs there, threatening to pour down upon us at any moment. The tree limbs bow with the weight of the moisture in the air. The crickets and cicadas are extra loud, the way they always are before it rains. The atmosphere is crackling with pent up electricity.

I've been up since dawn, prepping with Josiah. He's a big believer in finger flexing and hand exercises at times like this. He's a real pro when it comes to competitive worm fiddling. "You've got this, Lemon," he says. "You'll be the first queen in the history of this town. Your momma would be real proud."

The sleepy dirt roads of Break-A-Leg are positively swarming with activity. The front lawn of the high school has been turned into an arena for armadillo racing. Stalls line the streets, selling lemonade and fry bread and swamp cabbage stew. Uncle Obie has designated his palace grounds for overflow parking and is charging double the admission. Pretty much everyone in town has found some way to capitalize on the worm fiddling market. There are t-shirts and posters, plastic baggies filled with gummy worms and stuffed alligator children's toys. We get more visitors today than we do the entire rest of the year. As the reigning king, Uncle Josiah gives a few interviews to the local newspapers about what it means to be a cornerstone of folk tradition. His chest puffs up with pride as he looks over at me.

Sweets is slated to wrestle the Swamp Ghost just before my competition. There's a heavy turnout of Seminoles from the reservation this year just for that reason. I know this is important to Sweets. He's been looking forward to this moment since we were kids. Despite Josiah's advice about staying focused, I make my way over to the alligator-wrestling ring to watch.

Stanley Sweets and the Swamp Ghost have the crowd enthralled. I have to push my way past the throng of cheering onlookers to see. Sweets is shirtless and barefoot and his legs and feet are stained with mud. He's dancing around the Swamp Ghost, trying to wear her down as she swivels from side to side, snapping her mammoth jaws and hissing. She's a behemoth. A real prehistoric monster. Her creamy white flanks ripple and contract as she moves.

Sweets performs a simple frontal catch, holding her jaws closed with one hand, and the crowd goes wild. It's a simple enough move, but the Swamp Ghost bucks his hand, sweeps around and takes him down with her muscular tail. Sweets recovers himself and wrestles her into the submission position, sitting astride her back, his fingers forcing her eyes down into their bony sockets. He demonstrates a few of the old Seminole techniques for trussing and tying alligators before he gets down to the good stuff.

He pries her jaws open into the Florida Smile, a showy maneuver that displays all eighty of her giant teeth and the closed glottis valve at the back of her snowy white throat. Then he hooks his chin over the top of her snout and holds out both hands in the air. This leaves his head and neck completely exposed to her mercy. I hold my breath along with the crowd as he slowly extends his face between her massive jaws. The seconds seem to tick by into eternity. Mercifully, the Swamp Ghost holds her pose until the moment Sweets pulls his head back. Her jaws snap together with a staggering two thousand pounds of force. Enough to crush metal. The audience cheers and hoots. People begin chanting Sweets' name.

He stands there beside his alligator looking glorious and triumphant. He grins at the girls swooning in the stands. He waves at the shrieking children. Blows a kiss to his gran. He ignores me completely if he sees me at all, and suddenly I know that *this* is where Stanley Sweets will always want to be standing.

I trudge over to the fiddling grounds feeling as if my sneakers are lined with concrete.

"Everything go okay?" Josiah asks, and I nod.

Worm fiddling doesn't have the same pomp and glory of alligator wrestling. Still, there are banners and lanterns hung in the moss-draped trees. People have ringed the staked off squares of swampy turf with folding chairs and upturned buckets. Families have laid out plastic tarps on the ground where they can sit and watch us. We get into position as the commentator introduces each of us to the crowd. Then there's a little history on the tradition, function, and art of worm charming. I know this spiel by heart. Uncle Josiah helped write it.

"All right fiddlers," the announcer says. "Ready your stobs!"

There are a couple dozen of us. We all pound our stakes into the ground and wait.

"Ready. Set. Roop!"

The forest is filled with deafening vibrations, hums, groans and grunts as we furiously work our rooping irons. There is nothing quite like the sound of a swamp full of fiddlers. The crickets and cicadas take up our rhythms. The crowds tap their feet and cheer. The rain starts to fall. Each drop hits the ground to the beat of our fiddling.

I notice that Josiah is watching me more than he's watching his sticks. This is a classic rookie worm-charming mistake. Josiah knows better. He's trying to let me take the lead. But my heart just isn't in it. As the chorus of grunting crescendos, an older fellow from Texas that usually places second starts to lap us. His square of soil is glistening with worms. His eyes are closed. His weathered skin gleams with perspiration. I scan the crowd for Sweets, but he's nowhere to be found. My hands slip a couple of times and I completely lose my rhythm.

When the announcer calls time, we gather up our worms. I don't wait around for the counting. I can tell just by looking that I've lost. I turn in my buckets and leave my sticks on the ground.

"It's all right, Lemon," Uncle Josiah says, though his face betrays his encouraging words. "You'll get it next year."

•

I skip the Worm Fiddling Ball. I don't want to see Stanley Sweets and the pageant girl holding hands. I don't want to hear the platitudes of well-meaning Break-A-Leg folks trying to soften the blow of my colossal failure. I can't stomach the look in Uncle Josiah's eyes. Instead, I go home to Castle

Chinkapin and smash up Uncle Obie's half-finished paper-mâché tribute to the Swamp Ghost.

I sequester myself in my princess quarters and look out the window. Outside, the air is warm and vibrating with echoes of the day's fiddling. The cicadas and the crickets thrum with leftover melodies. The cypress trees quiver under the wind and rain, tapping against the glass in a mournful rhythm. The sad song of the whippoorwills punctuates the wet skies while, beneath it all, the alligators slide through the darkness, saturating the night with their deep, lovesick bellows.

ABOUT THE HIDING OF BURIED TREASURE

It's common enough to hear about the finding of buried treasure, but the real trick is in the hiding. The finding is easy. You just need some head lanterns, a pickaxe, an old sea-worn map, waterproof matches, a rune decoder, and possibly some dynamite and trip wire in case you're being shadowed. But hiding treasure is a lifelong toil.

Our island is chock-full of treasure, bursting at the seams with plunder and booty, trap doors, trick caves, and rocks marked with big mossy Xs. Pop has trained Jezebel and I to keep it hidden. We scrub the Xs off the rocks, cover hidden entrances with branches and hornets' nests, and fill the sunken mounds of old pirate graves until the earth is smooth. We do everything we can think of to throw visitors off the track. Pop plants fields of ragweed, sour grapes, wild garlic, and saw grass. He threads the trees with bramble vines and poisoned thorns. It was *his* Pop who let loose a plague of jumping spiders, giant rats, and polar bears upon our island many years ago—until the rats ate the jumping spiders and the polar bears ate the rats. We tried to train the polar bears to guard the treasure caves, but the animals have no interest in glittering, inanimate hordes. We keep them around anyway since they hypnotize the tourists with their moony pelts and silver fangs. They gobble them up from time to time, but it still doesn't stop people from coming.

In the winter, when the ground is frozen and the waves are funnels of ice, it's just us and the bears. Jezebel and I practice ice surfing while wearing crowns and tiaras, check our booby traps to make sure they're not frosted over, and search the island for new treasure for Pop to trade to other, friendlier islands. In the summer, there is no time to play. We are positively swarmed with visitors. People come here from all over. Their free-market noses are trained to follow the scent of wealth across oceans and deserts. It is the real story of humanity. They smile at us and sniff the air curiously. They look around at the tangled trees and spur-filled sands and invent convincing explanations for their visits.

"We just had to come see your charming island," they say, or, "We felt some draw to explore this part of the world." When the ground literally trembles with wealth, we tell visitors it's just the shifting of tectonic plates and the rumblings of a resident live volcano.

Pop grins at them from the docks, big holes in his mouth where he'd yanked his teeth out with a socket wrench. He's got a set of whalebone pirate falsies, chipped from chewing on gold coins, that he wears when we go into town on the mainland to trade. Jezebel and I can wear as many crowns and tiaras as we want in our wintry solitude, but when there are visitors on the island Pop likes us to seem dim-witted. Jezebel paints her lips in uneven red circles and kinks her orange hair with boxes of expired home perms. She talks with a slow drawl that has no place on a windswept northern island, but no one ever notices the farce. I keep a standard profile. I spin an old yoyo from one finger and blow giant spheres of bubble gum that burst on my cheeks. I never wash my hands or comb my hair.

Pop isn't our real Pop, and Jezebel isn't my real sister, but we feel like a family just the same. Pop found us—some might say rescued, some might say stole—from a mainland orphanage and raised us to be his pretend children.

·

I first see the balloon while I'm up in the lookout tower. Summer winds are never any good here. They always seem to blow things straight towards us whereas, the winter winds blow things away. The balloon is a big one, a fancy one, shaped like a medieval castle with elaborate turrets Its rainbow banners flap about in the sky. Whoever is inside it clearly does not know how to fly. It swoops and bumps across the breeze in crazy circles for a while, until eventually it trumpets in defeat and wedges itself into the spiky branches of one of our bramble trees, a good twenty feet off the ground. The nylon shell of the balloon bursts into cheerful confetti, while the thick gushing flame singes the leaves and sends the island's wombat-sized seagulls flying up into the air with loud caws.

I watch the man inside struggle to work out a way down before I get bored and wander off. Soon a boatload of people will arrive at Dead Man's Cove, so I scamper over there to make sure everything looks inhospitable and ugly. Jezebel and I arrange bleached whale bones in the sand and throw laxative-laced fish guts on the rocks so our ravenous birds will shit all over visitors while swooping and dive-bombing their picnic lunches of wine and marmalade sandwiches. When the visitors arrive I refuse to carry anyone's bags or help the high-heeled ladies across the sand. I deflect their curious questions with a surly scowl.

"Charlie," Jezebel whispers from behind a thorn bush. She is dressed like a pygmy today. Her orange hair is coated in mud and she has war paint smeared on her face. "Did you see the balloon in the trees?"

I nod. "He's stuck good. No getting out for a while."

"The colors," Jezebel says. "I've never seen anything like them."

She looks slightly bedazzled. I draw her attention to a couple of backpackers sharing a bag of granola, looking hardy and determined.

"There's no zip lining here," I call out to them. "No waterfall jumping. No rock climbing. No hang gliding. No swimming with dolphins. Just hungry bears and giant seagulls. If you get back in your kayaks and head south, you'll find an island with rainforests and elephants."

They eye me suspiciously, wander around the shore a little until their waterproof boots are caked in excrement and fish guts, then rinse themselves off and head back out to sea. As if on cue, one of our polar bears ambles out of the trees and sends the remaining tourists screaming for their vessels.

"That's an easy day's work," I say to Jezebel, tossing the bear a silver herring from my backpack. But when I turn around the bushes are empty and my sister has disappeared.

Jezebel is breathless over dinner. She hums with excitement, some secret girl-ness that I cannot understand. Pop doesn't notice. He sucks the meat out of crab legs, crushing the hard shells with his jaws. Butter and boiled seawater drip down his chin. Every now and again he breaks the silence to mutter something about the bloody tourists, or the plummeting price of jewel-encrusted crowns. Jezebel sighs into her dinner plate. She is sculpting balloon castles out of her potatoes.

•

The man stays up in his basket all summer. He's made a rope ladder he uses to crawl down when he wants to go fishing or swim in the ocean, but at night he seems perfectly content to sit in the wicker basket, grill fish over the open flame, and count stars through the wispy tatters of his balloon. He doesn't seem to be trying to get anywhere anytime soon.

Pop doesn't like him too much. "Simpleton," he says, watching from a pair of binoculars. Though he doesn't pay the man much more attention than that, one night he has me make a honey trail to the tree, hoping to attract the bears. Sometimes we have to do this sort of thing. Tourists consume our entire summers. They arrive in ocean-liners and jet planes. Sometimes helicopters drop parachuting squirrel gliders out over our private land. Once, an entire family beached themselves on our island, sun-swollen and half-starved, on a log raft they had built themselves. They kissed our cold shores like they had finally come home. They seemed surprised to find it was just sticks and sand. The look in their eyes was heartbreaking. I wanted to drop some jewels into their pockets as they pushed back off to sea, but Pop said no.

Ever since the ballooner caught Jezebel's eye, something is different with her. Girls are somewhat of a mystery, but I am a trained treasure hunter. I tap every surface of her room until I find a hollow spot in the floor. I shimmy the floorboard loose and find a peeling cigar box buried under a heap of tiaras and jewels. It is full of perfumed letters and declaratives. Lots of "I love you" and "I want be with you forever."

I try to tell Pop, but he can hardly hear anymore after taking so much booby-trap shrapnel in his ears. He is busy planning how to rig a decoy island across the bay, with fake treasure to distract the gold hunters for a while. "Don't bother me about yer sister's lady problems," he says. "Times are getting tough, Charlie. We gotta buckle down. Reinforce our perimeters. Tell that ducky to quit mooning over hot air balloons and help us keep this treasure hidden. That's what family is for."

That isn't what Jezebel seems to think anymore. She sits at the desk in her room making kaleidoscopes of gemstone chips and gold dust. In her journal she writes about plans to sell them in fancy galleries on the mainland. Every other page is about leaving our island.

"Charlie!" She jumps when she sees me standing in the doorway. One of her cheeks is shimmering iridescent where she must have touched her face.

"Jezebel," I say. "You have to forget the man in the balloon."

"What man in the balloon?" she asks, her skin turning an unattractive shade of plum. This is the trouble with girls. You can't trust them worth a dime.

"You're leaving us." I say. "Or you want to anyway. What has he said to make you want to abandon me and Pop?"

"Oh Charlie," she says, and her whole body shudders. "I'm not a kid anymore. I can't stay here forever. This is no kind of life for a woman."

With her frizzled hair and muddy clothes, Jezebel looks nothing like a woman to me. I tell her as much, and she throws me out of her room with all the strength of a born and bred treasure hider.

"I'm warning you, Charlie!" she yells through the door. I hear the slide of locks and clicks of latches. "Try infiltrating my personal space again and you'll be impaled by an eleventh century Viking sword!"

This is enough to make me cautious. Jezebel is a booby-trapping master, and she especially loves restoring ancient Scandinavian weapons. So I give up on her for now. Instead, I decide to go to the source of the problem and confront that Lotharian rake in the hot air balloon.

•

Pop is drunk on pirate rum, frying gull eggs in the dark kitchen. He's wearing a long pajama shirt and night vision goggles, and singing a shanty about adventure on the high seas. He doesn't even notice as I slip out the front door, exiting from a concealed fort cover made of sewn-up thorn branches and poison berry leaves.

I discover a worn footpath through the brush to the man's tree. I suspect my sister has carved it out. I tread in her footsteps quietly to avoid spooking any bats or bears or other nocturnal predators. I am almost to the site of their aerial love trysts when I make an amateur's error: I step into a trip line ankle snare and immediately find myself swinging back and forth, upside down, spiky brush snarling in my hair. This is Jezebel's handiwork, no doubt about it. It never occurred to me that she would booby trap the hot air balloon man from me and Pop, and this thought sends a piercing pain through me even as the blood rushes to my head.

But a treasure hider is never unprepared. I cut myself free with a dagger from my belt and tumble into a pile of thorn bushes. My ensuing howls alert the man in the balloon and, by the time I've righted myself, he has climbed down his rope ladder and is standing before me.

"Charlie," he says. He is pretty plain, up close. He smiles and his slightly crooked teeth glow white in the moonlight.

"Sorry about the trap." He holds out a hand to me. "Your

sister insisted. She was worried your Pop would try to slit my throat while I slept."

I shake his hand cautiously. It is calloused from climbing and fishing.

"Pop *would* slit your throat if he knew what you were trying to steal," I tell him.

The man looks at the dagger in my hand and nods. "I'm Nigel," he says. His expression remains friendly. He gestures to the rope ladder. "Want to come up? We can pull out some of those thorns."

I don't like the implication that I need his help for anything. He is a thieving, good-for-nothing hot air ballooner as far as I'm concerned, but I do want to see what he's got in his basket, so I follow him up, pulling thorns with my teeth and spitting them into the night as I climb.

Nigel's balloon basket looks pretty ordinary. There are some blankets, disrupted from sleep, a pile of books that have seen better days, a string of dried fish hanging from a rack, old moonshine jugs filled with water, and smaller baskets, woven out of vines, containing fruit and other foraged foods like garlic bulbs and wild onions. From the top of his tree the stars look extra bright. Nigel lights his lantern and motions for me to have a seat.

"So," he says.

"So," I say.

"About your sister."

"You can't have her,"

This leaves us in silence for a few minutes. I eye him up good and continue to spit thorns so he knows I mean business. Somewhere in the forest the trees shake with tussling polar bears rummaging for dinner. A colony of bats is dislodged and they skitter off over our heads. Nigel doesn't flinch. I suppose he's become used to this sort of thing.

"Charlie, you can't keep her here forever." He sounds suspiciously like Jezebel.

"Is that what you've been telling her?" I ask, trying to keep the anger out of my voice. "No one is keeping her here. This is *our* island. It's where we belong!"

"People belong where they want to be," Nigel says softly, like he's afraid his words will bring my world crashing down around me.

I could kill him. Well, maim him at least. He has the nerve that only an infiltrator can have. "Go land on your own island and say that," I say, grabbing his jugs of water and throwing them off the side of the basket. They shatter on the ground below. "These are our jugs and you can't drink from them." I toss the fruit overboard as well. "This is our food you have taken."

He doesn't look particularly guilty. In fact he's taken on the patient expression of an adult trying to calm a small child. "I'm an explorer," he says. "The world is mine."

There's a pile of cloth folded up to one side with sewing needles and thread. He's repairing his turrets and, by the looks of it, he will be airborne again soon. The thought of Jezebel sailing away with him strikes real panic in me.

"All right," I say. "You can have some treasure. Gold, silver, diamonds. I will bring you whatever you want. Just leave my sister behind."

He shakes his head at me. "You can't blame a girl for wanting to see the world," he says. "And you can't blame a guy for falling in love with your sister."

I should shank him. I know I should, but I can't. Tears, hot and fat, well up in my eyes. I try to muster up some righteous anger. Anger that will make me ready to slit Nigel's throat. But nothing comes. All I can think about is summers without Jezebel. Winters without her. Nighttime ramblings and booby-trapping without her. Before I can stop them, the tears are falling. Pop would be disgusted.

I hop out of the balloon basket and scale the ladder before Nigel has time to react. I race through the forest, oblivious to traps and tripwires and wandering polar bears. I'm going to tell Pop. I'll let him do what I can't. But when I reach the house, Pop is passed out across the kitchen table, his night vision goggles slipped to one side. He is snoring loud enough to bring the walls down. I knock on Jezebel's door but she doesn't answer. Back in my room I pull treasure boxes of jewels and coins from the back of my closet and run my fingers through them, trickling emeralds and rubies all over the floor. Nestled in velvet is an ornate golden crown and scepter. Jezebel has the matching tiara. When we were younger we used to dress up in fur cloaks and call ourselves the King and Queen of Frozen Island. Pop would clap his hands and laugh while we ordered the sea gulls around like subjects and made grand speeches to the winter sea. We even had Pop officiate a marriage ceremony one winter, before we were old enough to learn that even pretend brothers and sisters didn't do that sort of thing.

I don the crown and head back to Jezebel's room, pounding on the door and screaming for her to open up. Jezebel had sworn she would stay with me forever. I kick and claw and shout, but it's no use. Then I do the most shameful thing I have ever done. I lean up against my sister's door and cry myself to sleep with my favorite crown on.

•

In the morning, it is Pop who shakes me awake. "Come see, Charlie! That pickle-brained dope has finally left the island."

I shake doubloons off me and take off my crown.

"Wake up your sister," he says, swigging from a mug of rum before heading back out into the clear morning.

I don't bother to knock on Jezebel's door. I follow Pop down to the beach, where tourists are lined up along the water's edge for a good look. The castle has been patched up, the turrets erected into the chilly morning air. It is a cold wind—the first wind of winter—that makes the crowd shiver and gives speed to the monstrous balloon.

Pop's eyes aren't too good, but I know he sees the shock of orange hair that is Jezebel. She is waving goodbye to us from above the ocean.

For a moment Pop is speechless, and then he breaks into such a terrible fit of obscenities and vulgar threats that the last of the summer treasure hunters pack up their belongings and make for the sea.

Pop is inconsolable. He rants. He raves. He fights a polar bear. He breaks everything in the house until there's nothing left and he's forced to go outside and tear trees straight out of the ground. He goes on a rum bender for a week. I do my best to avoid him for most of this time.

Then, one day, when the wind is cold but the frost has yet to arrive, he disappears. He takes the good boat that we hide in a cave at the southern tip of the island. I don't know where he's gone—to sell treasure, or maybe to rescue Jezebel. I stare at the sky for hours, for days, looking for colored banners and streamers on the horizon with a spyglass, but I don't find any. I try to keep to my usual routine of checking traps, exploring caves, counting the treasure that will one day be mine. Still, I can't help but feel like the island is empty despite its hidden, glittering mounds. At my most desperate, I take the boxes of home perms and hair dye out of Jezebel's room and stack them in neat piles beside my bed, as if they'll manifest a new sister while I sleep.

•

When Pop reappears he is not alone. He pulls the boat right up onto the sand at Dead Man's Cove and jumps ashore, his chest thrown out like he's staking a claim.

"Charlie!" he calls, and I rush down to greet him. He spits out his pirate falsies and puts them in his pocket. "Get us some rum. We're having a celebration!"

A girl with huge eyes climbs out of the boat from behind him. She is smaller than Jezebel, younger too. In her hands are gems, tons of them, glittering different colors in the pale sunlight.

"Meet your new sister, Calliope. Calliope, this here's Charlie. He's going to teach you all about wolf traps and squirrel snares and hangman's nooses."

Calliope smiles at me. "Hello."

"Nice to meet you," I say, eyeing her good. I imagine what she'd look like with her hair permed up, mud streaked on her face.

Pop's already left us behind. He's in high spirits and heads straight to the house for a jug of rum. Calliope waits patiently as I finish pulling the boat up, out of reach from the tide. Her patent leather shoes sink slightly into the sand.

"Is it true this island is full of treasure?"

"All kinds of treasure," I say. "Anything you could ever dream." At her silence I add, "You're gonna love it here. We never have to go to school. And I'll show you how to ice skate and build snow castles." The words don't sound completely right yet. There is still something hollow about them to my ears. But when Calliope turns her blue eyes up to mine, I feel a surge of brotherly protection, and the terrible loneliness that has consumed me since Jezebel abandoned us begins to recede. I smile at my new sister. "Do you like tiaras?"

She nods and smiles shyly at me.

"That's great," I say.

Calliope slips her hand in mine as we follow Pop's footprints in the sand.

BABA YAGA'S HOUSE OF FORGOTTEN THINGS

The grannies don't sleep much. They sit on their porches and rock through the night, setting a hair-raising rhythm with the clickety-clack of their knitting needles and the wet, juicy chomping of their toothless gums. These noises have a way of stopping a teenage libido right in its tracks. Girls and boys bunk together here and there has never been any incident yet. Between the old-lady sounds that accompany our every waking moment, the undignified quality of most granny-approved activities, and the combined weight of their judgmental stares, our hormones are pretty well neutralized.

Which can make this a difficult place to foster a crush. It's hard work overcoming the ambience here. It smells of old mothballs and denture cream, and the evening breeze is paper dry. The breeze doesn't so much relieve the heat as it coats your skin with a fine dusting of baby powder. It blows through open windows, stopping to dip its fingers in jars of rose and lavender scented talcum left sitting out on the sills. Sometimes I wake up with sore throats that taste like flowers. Sometimes I hear Frankie sneeze as he dreams.

Trieste and I tap messages to each other on the tin roof that lies over our heads. It is a language we learned from the summer rains.

"I miss cigarettes," Trieste taps.

"I miss my friends," I reply.

"I miss my boyfriend," she taps back.

When she taps that, I don't respond. I only stare at the corrugated tin in the moonlight and listen to the squeak-clack-chomp of the grannies in the night.

•

Trieste is here because she stole her parents' car, crashed it into a tree, and hit a pedestrian in the process. She isn't even old enough to drive. The rest of us are only guilty of things like bad grades, drinking underage, being disrespectful to our families, or shit-bombing houses. Small things. Trieste has the most serious record of any of us delinquents. There is a certain bad-ass pride in the way she walks—saunters, more like—or the way she flips her hair, sending it honey-buzzing in the sunlight. It is hard not to be impressed with her.

In the morning, when Granny Nickel rounds us up to put us in the chain gangs, I position myself so that I am linked to Trieste. It is not only because her voice is surprisingly sweet when she sings, it is also because I like to watch her work.

We have all kinds of chores here, but right now we are doing the planting for the grannies' gardens. It is a relief to replace the old lady smells with the vibrant scent of hot tomato vines and ripe strawberry fields. Insects hum in the grass and clouds graze up in the sky. Except for the iron shackle on my foot, I could almost imagine this is something I like to do.

Granny Nickel catches me watching Trieste's shoulders, gleaming with sweat as she hoes, and whacks me good with her steel-tipped cane.

"Rutabagas, cabbages, turnips," Frankie says in a low voice. "Who eats this shit?"

"The grannies do," Trieste answers tartly. "It keeps them regular."

Frankie wrinkles his nose. He does not like the thought of granny bodily functions. He's the newest delinquent. His face still blanches at liver spots and pickled beets. He eyes the knitting needles suspiciously and blows raspberries as Granny Nickel turns her back to us and walks away. Frankie is a hard shell.

"Disgusting," he says.

Trieste shrugs and continues to hoe.

Granny Nickel is drinking a glass of gin and lemonade, smoking a grape cigar, and knitting. She is the toughest granny by far. She looks like a starving greyhound, but swells of muscle pop out of her dress sleeves. She loves having arm wrestling contests in the evenings. She can still beat the strongest of us boys. Her rocking chair is set up in the shade and a pile of knitting spills out across the grass beside it. Even her yarn looks steely. Rumor has it that she spins the barbwire fences that surround the camp.

"Quit yapping!" she yells at Frankie without dropping a stitch. Her knitting needles flash in the sunlight. "Unless you want to start singing in rounds again."

This shuts Frankie up. It's hard being new here. I've taken Frankie under my wing. In real life he lives with his sister in the suburbs of Philly. She sent him to The Old Crone's Boot Camp because he was having behavioral problems at school. Myself, I'm here for duct-taping a boy to the wall of the gymnasium. After getting caught smoking behind the garage, and sticking bananas in the principal's tailpipe, the duct-taping was the last straw for my parents. As soon as the school year ended, they shipped me off to the crones.

Granny camp is the newest fad in the treatments of delinquents, especially those of us who come from broken homes or have problems respecting authority. The grannies get the entire summer to whip us into shape and instill the values they believe are lacking in these god-less times. They can be mean and vindictive. Angry from years of being mistreated and forgotten about. Ornery with the toil of growing old.

"It is not enough to just respect your elders," Granny Melon tells us fairly often. "You must always remember to fear them as well."

She's not kidding either. Granny Nickel likes to sneak up on us in the middle of the night with her teeth out, sit on our chests, and let her silver hair tickle our faces until we open our eyes. This is called "boo-hagging." You don't know fear until you have a warty, deflated bag of skin hanging over you in the dark, and the lonely smell of dying crawling up your nose. It gives you bad dreams for weeks. Granny Nickel is relentless. The more you scream, the more she stalks you. She won't leave you alone until you learn to quake silently with respect.

•

Baba Yaga is the supreme matriarch of this geriatric hell. She's the biggest, the oldest, and the ugliest of the grannies, and she is only called upon to deal with the most extreme cases of insubordination. She lives separate from the other grannies in a stilted house with laminated playing cards for roof shingles and a pathway made of hockey pucks, Scrabble tiles, and old dentures. Just the threat of her is enough to make the bravest boy quiver. Part of the terror comes from the fact that she is rarely seen. To us, she is a misshapen, hulking shadow seen through the lacy curtains of her windows, or a monstrous silhouette riding her pet pig through the forest at night.

On hot days, like today, the grannies skinny dip in the pond behind their cottages. You can tell this is what they're doing when you see the ducks come streaming out of the water in a steady line. None of us ever try to sneak up on them. Rather, we hide in the scrub pines that surround our tin shacks and pretend not to hear them calling for us to help peel the leeches from their vein-ribboned legs. We watch through the trees as Granny Melon comes out in the nude, grabs two poorly hidden kids by their ears, and leads them back to help with the leech removal.

"Jesus," Frankie says, shaking his head and looking pale. "This is hell on earth."

Trieste pulls out a grape cigar she pilfered from Granny Nickel's knitting bag, and we all take turns dragging on it in our shelter of trees. She's also brought some of the stationary the grannies provide for us to write letters home. It usually features puppies or kittens. "I'm making a map," she says proudly.

"For what?" Frankie and I both ask at the same time.

"To escape, of course." She shows us how she has been recording the boundaries of the grannies' property. "Right here," she says, pointing to a line of hedges behind the silk flower gardens and the cemetery. "Beside Baba Yaga's house. I think there might be a road of some sort."

Just the idea of it makes me feel queasy. Rutabaga-beet stew threatens to repeat on me.

Frankie's eyes are fervent. His cheeks are as pink as the insides of watermelons. "Escape?" He seems to have latched on to that word.

"Baba Yaga," I say.

Trieste picks junebugs from the hem of her skirt and looks

completely calm. To keep a poker face while suggesting we defy these hell-witches means that she is either a complete sociopath or the bravest person I know. In the distance we hear the shrieks of the kids pulling leeches. Frankie is no longer shuddering. He stares at Trieste as if she is the only way out of here. Lately, Granny Nickel has taken to boo-hagging him relentlessly.

"You have to promise," Trieste says, eyeing me particularly. "You can't breathe a word of this to anyone. Nickel would have us plucking chickens and massaging bunions for the rest of the summer."

I nod. I will do anything for Trieste, even if it means agitating the grannies. Even though I don't think we stand much chance of orchestrating an escape.

After supper, Granny Melon calls me aside. It's as if they can hear my traitor thoughts echoing through the mess hall. Melon is as soft and round as Nickel is thin and hard. She really looks like a grandma, too. She smells like butterscotch and lilacs, and her white hair poofs out into summertime clouds. It's deceptive, though. She's quick and has a fiery temper, and she is not above chasing you through the fields with a cement-filled rolling pin when you do wrong.

"Clive," she says, beckoning me over with a pruned fingertip. "You barely touched your food tonight. Is something wrong?"

"No," I say. I feel Trieste's eyes on me. "Nothing really. I guess I just miss home."

Granny Melon pats my head and looks pleased. "That's good. You should miss your home." She digs around in the pockets of her faded housedress until she produces some puppy stationary. "Write your parents a letter tonight," she says. Before I can finish exhaling, she shatters my relief.

"When you finish, bring it out to the veranda and read it to us so we can check your progress."

She shoos me with a swat that nearly knocks me off my feet before turning her attention to a group of kids who are supposed to be cleaning up the mess hall. One unfortunate boy gets clobbered on the head with the rolling pin before I make it outside to meet Trieste.

The sun is just setting. The long grasses are lit up with blinking fireflies, and a few of the younger kids are trying to catch them and smoosh them into a glowing paste.

"That's juvenile," Trieste says as we walk past. It is enough to make them all look ashamed and guilty. I am proud to be at her side.

"I have to write a letter home," I tell her. "And present it to the grannies tonight on the veranda. I told Melon I was homesick."

"That's perfect." Trieste's eyes are twin beacons of freedom. Her hair swings around her shoulders, scooping up the summer moonlight. I can barely stop myself from professing my love.

"You can provide the distraction," she says. "Frankie and I will do recon on the silk flower gardens. I know there has to be a way out through there."

I'm not big on the idea of her and Frankie carrying out our first mission without me. "I'm not sure what I can write in a letter home to my parents that will distract them for that long."

"Listen, Clive," she says, leaning in so close I can smell the parsnip casserole on her breath. "I picked you because you're smart. You'll figure it out."

I can't help myself. I have to ask. "What did you pick Frankie for?"

"Because he'll do whatever I tell him to." She smiles like

we are alone in this secret. Behind her the fireflies are blinking out S.O.S. messages.

·

My letter home is a masterpiece. In it, I praise the grannies for their commitment to terrorizing us kids. I describe the long talcum filled nights, the sound of bullfrogs and the relentless clickety-clack of steel knitting needles, the whimpering of the other delinquents. I reflect upon the odiousness of my previous wrong doings. I pontificate about the value of good hard work, respect, discipline and, above all, fear. The fear part is no exaggeration. My voice quakes as I begin reading aloud.

The assembled grannies sit in a line of rocking chairs and eye me with wet, slurpy stares. There are lots of grannies here that I have never seen before. Grannies made of crepe paper and bone. Some are little more than ghosts of self-righteous indignation. They are all present except for Baba Yaga.

I conclude my letter with a genuinely heartfelt appeal to return home to my family. I get so caught up in my own fervor there are even tears in my eyes as I finish. Then silence. I am suspended in the opaque stares of thick-rimmed bifocals and squinty, cataract-clouded eyes. It is impossible to gauge their reactions. I wait for somebody to clap or say something.

"Sissyboy," hisses one of grannies. Her flaccid skin looks like boiled chicken.

Melon whaps her with the rolling pin. She's partial to me. I can tell.

"You did a nice job, Clive," she says. "Even if you have a tendency to wax poetic."

There is a smattering of bored and brittle applause, and

then some grannies disappear into the recesses of the dark while others pick up knitting needles and continue their evening routines.

"Okay," Melon says. "I think you're ready."

"For what?" I ask. I'm thinking about Trieste and Frankie crawling together through the disintegrating scraps of silk flowers. I hope it's muddy out there. I know how seductive she can be in the moonlight.

Granny Melon leads me by the ear to the part of the camp where the night is deepest. Ahead of us, the outline of a house sits high on stilts that look like clean-picked chicken legs. Piles of hockey pucks and old Scrabble tiles catch the pale moonlight, their bleak gleam lighting the way. An owl hoots out some haunting and insidious warning. A pig snorts in the darkness. The cicadas click like old bones. I follow Melon's crumpled footsteps. The fusty smell of roses settles upon us as we walk. A pair of old dentures bites into the sole of my sneaker. These are the things that nightmares are made of.

"Come on," Granny Melon says as my steps falter. "We're not getting any younger." A far away cackle raises the gooseflesh on my arms.

I think of Trieste. Trieste is out there somewhere searching the boundaries of the silk flower gardens for our way to freedom. I think of her cool calm, her incandescent beauty, her infallible fearlessness. I think of her secret messages tapped out to me in the darkness of the shack. I climb the rickety stairs, step onto the front stoop of Baba Yaga's porch, and hold steady. I am doing this for the girl I love.

"Knock," says Melon, before disappearing into the discordant noise of the insects of the night.

I don't have to knock. My hand is lifted only halfway when the door swings open to reveal the ruler of this antediluvian camp for troubled teens. The supreme matriarch in all her girdled glory. Huge and hulking, with sagging pockets of flesh, and soft wrinkles like sad spiderwebs bowing beneath the weight of ancient cocoons, connecting her pulpy features: eyes to ears, nose to mouth. She cultivates a mustache and beard that would be the envy of most guys my age. She gives me a slow sweep of her shadowy eyes and waves me forward, silencing the crickets and bending an awestruck breeze through the potted plants on the veranda.

Trieste, I think. She's out there somewhere navigating bravely. I channel her fearlessness into my jellied knees. One step forward. Two steps. I follow the sweeping muumuu train of Baba Yaga's housecoat, the tattered patterns of polyester peacocks that lap the dust behind her feet.

"Clive," she says. "I have a job for you."

I'm imagining pickling the limbs of small children or pulling the legs off spiders one by one for a stew. I have no thoughts of defying her. Whatever the job is, I'm ready.

"Very rarely does anyone see this room," she continues. "But Nickel and Melon see something special in you." She stops and hovers over me, as if searching for whatever it is the other grannies see. Her eyes are sloe black and squinched together beneath drooping eyelids. Her eyebrows are spiky tufts of suspicion. I'm dwarfed by her horrible majesty. I shrivel under her stare.

Trieste, I think.

Baba Yaga just barely clears the doorway ahead of me. I follow her into the room and blink. Try not to sneeze. And blink.

All around us quiver mountains of dusty hoard, the room

filled floor to ceiling with antiquated odds and ends the likes of which I've never seen before. There are old dresses, broken clothespins, eyeless ragdolls, worn-out school desks, dusty photo albums, rusted watering cans, jam jars filled with marbles, paper birds on sticks, and gilded picture frames with glass cracked and smoked from age. I am in the treasure den of some magnificent monster.

"Something in here is yours," she says. She lets out a deep, wet cough resplendent with flying spittle. "Your job is to find it."

"I'm sorry?" I say. She can't possibly mean for me to search through all these heaps without telling me what I'm looking for.

Suddenly the house lurches and groans, and the hoard quivers anew. I am terrified at the thought of being buried alive beneath the mountains of junk.

"Is this house moving?" I ask.

Baba Yaga's face creases into what I think might be a smile. "It smells trouble." She cackles a little and coughs another phlegmy cough. "But don't you worry about that, boy. You begin your search."

In my months here at granny camp, I have run through a variety of emotions, most of them varying shades of fear, but nothing has come close to the terror of being interred in a chicken-footed shack with Baba Yaga herself while my friends are crawling around in the mud somewhere without me.

The jostling of the room brings a showering of old magazines down over my head. The house is on the prowl and it occurs to me that it might be looking for Trieste. One magazine falls open to reveal a cigarette ad from decades ago, a Marlboro man leaning up against an old pickup truck. I kick it gently to the side and make my way toward the middle of the room.

There are deliberate goat paths made through the mess. I follow them carefully, my nerves jumping with every lurch and movement of the house. I trip on the hem of an old communion dress and dislodge a frisky jack in the box, which causes a hillock of junk to topple to the ground. I topple as well, now swimming in a sea of old remnants, forgotten things stored away for some reason I don't understand. I paddle around trying to find a footing or a handhold. Brittle fabrics crumble beneath me. Wood splinters. I catch a mason jar filled with buttons just before it shatters against a cracked mirror. A moth-eaten mink stole, eyes and teeth intact, pops up in front of me and suddenly a memory is shaken loose from my mind.

An old mink farm. Abandoned cages. A large, two-story house at the end of a swirling stretch of dirt driveway framed with Queen Anne's lace and bluebells. A pond in front with lily pads, water lilies that open and close with the sun. A fishing dock. A log raft. A rose garden full of soft, ripe blossoms as big as my hands. An evergreen forest leading off into acres of dark, enchanted woods. Polish voices, clipped and sometimes caring.

I stare at the dead mink, transfixed. As the house rolls, up comes a plastic cube with pictures stuck on every side. There is the memory. I can see it on the grainy photo paper. An old farm, and a red brick house with big bay windows. The cube flips over and I recognize my father, as a young man, chopping down saplings in a faded afternoon long ago. Another jolt and the picture cube jumps off into the roiling mess and other things pop up in its place. Microscope slides of bugs and leaves. Fried green pepper sandwiches and tumblers of cheap scotch. Old vases and tarnished silver. Hand-knit dolls that double as toilet paper cozies.

Still the memories are coming. Riding an old tractor through an enchanted woods. Pulling up eggplants from the moist earth. Catching turtles from the pond and scrubbing their backs with toothbrushes. Counting stars. Catching air in a glass jar to take home at the end of the summer.

I see my grandmother's face now, pruned and bulbous from a life of farm labor. "You're such a funny child. Eugene! Come see! Clive is catching air in jam jars."

They laugh at me, both of them. My grandmother and my grandfather. The summer air is lacy and gold. I don't mind that they laugh. I am trapping a piece of that summer so I never lose it.

The house surges up, as if spewed by some ancient memory well. A little jar, meant for strawberry jam, and sealed tight against the years, glitters in the dusty air. That's my childhood in there. I make a flying leap off an old baby carriage, scurry up a broken ladder, and grab at the jar before it disappears, holding it tightly as the house continues to jostle back and forth. I take shelter under an old canoe and brace myself against falling debris, squeezing my eyes shut against the assault of lost memories.

When everything stills and the door finally opens, Baba Yaga finds me huddled beneath the canoe, clutching my old jam jar, my cheeks wet with tears. She doesn't look any less terrible to me.

"Did you find what you were supposed to?" she asks.

I nod. I think I want to thank her, but I don't dare. I brush cobwebs from my hair and step out from under the canoe. The room has rearranged itself. It's still a mess, but there are new goat paths now, curling out in different directions.

"I found something too." Baba Yaga smiles. It is terrible

to behold. "Security breach," she says. "Two campers escaped. Almost never happens. There was a rabbit hole through the fence in the silk flower gardens. You can believe we'll be tightening up surveillance around here."

I nod and follow her back out to the front porch. When I get to the top step, Baba Yaga kicks me down the stairs with a pointed heel and cackles.

I end up in a pile of shit, face to face with her giant pig. It gives me a disinterested snort as I get up and start back toward my cabin. The air is filled with the screams of campers. Ghostly white figures dart past me in numbers quicker than I can count. The security breach has the ground trembling and the trees shaking. The grannies have abandoned their knitting needles and are boo-hagging in full force. Trieste and Frankie may have escaped, but the rest of the campers are paying for their infraction. I try not to think about how Frankie is probably watching the moonlight tangle with her hair right now. Or how silent the roof will be without her night time messages. A lilac scented breeze whispers through the air and I steel my resolve and hold on to the jam jar in my pocket.

HOW TO GET RID
OF A GHOST

& OTHER LESSONS FROM
CAMP PISPOGUTT

It's lucky that Pispogutt rhymes with lots of things. I have the campers close their eyes and make up rhymes about camp while I hide Russian nesting dolls around the perimeter of the nature cabin. The game isn't over until every nesting doll has been rescued from makeshift shelters of moss and slippery elm bark. Sometimes I throw other wildcards into the treasure hunt. Indian pipes. Forget-me-nots. Hemlock sprigs. This is my fallback exercise for when I'm too hung over to think up anything original. Which is nearly every day.

I try not to talk to my ghost in front of other people. This morning I don't even want to look at her. Last night she kept me up for hours with the clickety-clack of her silver knitting needles. I know she's pissed about being ignored, because when I take the children out to the fire circle to practice building fires she keeps blowing out the tiny flames. I tell the campers to keep up the good work before I sneak inside the cabin for a quick slug of vodka.

"You've got a drinking problem," my ghost says, materializing in the doorway. The air between us turns frosty. "There's little kids playing with fire unchaperoned out there."

"You're my problem," I tell her. I've dribbled a little vodka down my shirt, which bears the proud Camp Pispogutt logo in a bright, hopeful canary yellow. Just beneath it is a rising sun.

My ghost turns from the doorway and walks to the maple outside, pulls herself up into the tall branches and twirls around. She laughs. "Tell it to your therapist. Better yet, explain it to your boss. Spill the beans and see who believes you."

She's still laughing. I go back outside just in time. One of the younger kids has figured out how to get a pile of leaves to smolder with a magnifying glass and a shard of sunlight.

My boss is a large, formerly Jewish, recently converted Zen Buddhist called Bear. He has a five-year plan to turn Camp Pispogutt into a mindfulness meditation retreat for families. I know this because he showed me his dream manifestation board during my initial interview. At our camp training he had Doshinji monks come down from the Catskills and stay the weekend so we could all learn how to be attuned to our surroundings. They had names like Brother Sun and Sister Smile. They took us on a lot of slow walks through the forest.

"Imagine your feet are kissing the earth with each step," Brother Sun would say.

I staggered along, drunk as could be, wondering why the monks couldn't see my ghost. It seemed like a renegade angry spirit was the kind of thing they should be attuned to. On the last day of their visit I broke down on a yoga mat and confessed my sins to Brother Sun.

I guess confessing to Doshinji monks is nothing like confessing to a Catholic priest. I begged for help, for penance, a rite of reconciliation, but he was a kind wall of brown-robed detachment. "You need to clear your mind of impurities," he said. "There is energy. There is the spirit. We create personal versions of this."

It was the first and only time I mentioned my ghost to another person.

Of course, *she* heard the whole thing. She was furious and didn't speak to me for days. Silent treatment from a ghost doesn't sound bad, but it can be the most nerve-wracking form of haunting.

·

My ghost especially loves the nature cabin. It's full of the husks of dead things—butterflies, beetles, birds, and the skulls and vertebrae of all sorts of animals, from mice to muskrats to giant elk. It's a bone yard of the living, breathing forest outside. I teach the campers about our surroundings by tracing outward from what's left behind. My ghost is always stealing the bones. I pretend not to notice so we don't have to talk about why she does this. On good days she sits on the nature cabin's splintery counters and follows my lessons with some interest. On the bad days, like today, she torments me and plays pranks on the campers.

After lessons in the cabin we go out and explore nature. I've got a pretty strong buzz going when a group of campers spots a nest with perfect sky-blue robin's eggs in it. I pretend to be thrilled. Once I really would have been. Now I hardly notice the colors or the teacup china quality to the eggs. Instead I'm glaring at my ghost, who is tying two campers' shoelaces together. The girls trip and bump their heads on their way to the ground. I make a play of trying to find the culprit before convincing everyone it was all in good fun. We move on to catching newts and salamanders.

"Finally," my ghost says, hanging upside down from a tree branch as we turn over logs and splash through streams. "Thank god you're not harvesting butterfly eggs today. I am so sick of watching you scrape milkweed with plastic spoons. At least these things move."

Her blond hair dangles in baby-fine wisps that snake out to taste the air. I want to tell her she doesn't have to hang around and watch all the time, but I can't yell at her in front of the campers. "Please," I hiss. "Please go away." I turn my attention to a little girl who's balanced on a rotten log. "There are living things that need my help right now."

·

I blame a lot on her. Things happen. Things that seem like omens, or something worse. Birds fly into the screened windows of cabins, batting their beaks against the wire mesh, poking holes for swarms of mosquitoes to fly in. Someone puts tadpoles in the Kool-aid. I find a hognose snake in the cabin, mistake it for a copperhead, and sever its head with a shovel in front of some campers before realizing my error. Juniper, the much beloved, injured flying squirrel we're taking care of, gives birth and eats her own kits.

I can't prove she's behind it, but I know she is.

One day there is a thunderstorm so fierce we all have to crowd inside the small, rickety nature cabin. In the pitching shadows and rumbling darkness of the storm it feels like we're in a ship. My ghost crawls around the ceiling, knocking mice nests and excrement from the rafters onto our heads. The kids scream. They panic. They jostle terrariums full of newts and spiders. I have to radio down to the main office for backup. My ghost looks pleased at my inability to handle the situation.

"You're an asshole," I say. We glare at each other.

In life we weren't like this. In life we were friends.

Bear sends up one of the lifeguards, who takes in the scene with some horror. I have the five- and six-year-olds this afternoon. In their distress they squash newts and trample bird bones beneath the soles of their sneakers. I can't blame them. My ghost is breathing on the backs of their necks. The whites of their little eyes roll around with terror.

"Christ, Regan," the lifeguard says. His name is Bay and he's worked here a few summers now. A lot of the staff began as former counselors. They're a tight clique. There's no room for a girl and her ghost. "It's like a horror movie in here. Let's just take them down to the mess hall and wait out the worst of it."

The mess hall is an open-air pavilion with plenty of benches and no specimen jars or poisonous animals. It's not the safest shelter during a thunderstorm, but I don't argue with him. We do a head count, pair the kids up, and Bay takes the front while I hold up the rear of the line. My ghost trails through the rain after us, laughing at the thunder and holding her palms up toward the sky.

"You've got circles under your eyes," Bay says.

The kids have calmed down. A few of the smaller ones huddle against us, but for the most part it's turned into an adventure for them. Bay is tall and strong and brings an aura of official lifeguard safety wherever he goes. When we arrive at the pavilion, the campers forget their recent trauma and run around the picnic tables playing tag.

"Really, you look like shit," he says, ear-muffing the little boy beside him. "Maybe you should see the nurse, or at least move back into the cabins."

We're sitting on the top of a picnic table now as the spray of cold rain bounces off the grass and mists over us. My ghost is dancing out there, spinning in circles, her thin dress stuck to her body, delighting in the heavy thunder cracks and white bolts that zigzag over the trees.

There's nothing a nurse can do for me. The cabins are no good, either. All the other specialists and instructors share cabins. The counselors share cabins with the campers. I stay in my own tent at the edge of Beaver Pond. It's isolated from the rest of the camp and hidden from view by Big Poppa, a giant rocky precipice that is off limits to the campers. Bear agreed to this because I told him it was part of my solitary journey to attain spiritual enlightenment. Really I just need a place where, for a few hours each day, I can stop pretending my dead friend isn't following my every move. Pretending I don't need liquor to make it manageable. Pretending I'm not falling apart.

"I'm fine," I finally say. "I like sleeping out in the open. Those cabins make me claustrophobic."

In the evenings, after camp lessons are over, Bay and the others sit out by the lake and socialize. Their voices carry over the water and to my campsite. They tell each other stories about their days. They have nicknames for everyone, the kids, the directors, but I don't know who is who.

After another long silence, I ask Bay: "Do I have a nickname?"

He laughs. "A nickname? No, but you should."

"Dances with Salamanders," I say.

"Swims with Muskrats."

"Flies with Bats."

Travels with Ghost.

She's beside me now, her dress transparent on her skin. Raindrops hang off her eyelashes. "Say it," she urges, her lips curved into a half moon. "Say Travels with Ghost." She leans across me and holds her face so close to Bay's that their noses almost touch. "That's why she doesn't sleep in the cabins. Because she has me."

Bay shivers and rubs at the gooseflesh spreading across his arms. "I think you're becoming feral," he says. "You're spending too much time with children and wild animals."

"She's a drunk," my ghost informs him.

"You should try being around a group of your peers." He smiles. "It really doesn't hurt."

"Says Mr. Lifeguard," she says with a sigh. "Do you want me to tell you how many of the counselors he's slept with? You're killing me, Regan. You used to be smart and fun." She launches herself away from us and back into the storm, doing cartwheels and back handsprings.

"I'm fun," I tell Bay. "Last week I made up a song about a butterfly named Omoscis who drinks nectar with his proboscis. The campers loved it."

Bay does his best to feign amusement.

If Bay could see my ghost he would be awestruck. When she was alive she was stunning. As a ghost she is magnificent. All glowing and golden and long-limbed. Ethereal. At least that's the way she looks when she knows I'm watching her. Sometimes, when she thinks I'm sleeping, I see her drawn up in a corner of my tent like a crouching spider while she knits. It usually takes me at least a half pint of vodka before I can fall asleep to the clicking rhythm of her gleaming ghost needles.

•

Every time I am radioed to come down to the main office, I'm sure someone will notice that I'm drunk. I try to be discreet. I sneak off to town for booze, then transfer my stash into water bottles before returning to camp. I cover my scent with loads of insect repellent and hand sanitizer, to the point that my flesh should be peeling off. And I swim.

I swim a lot. I like to watch Bay, and I like the smell of lake water drying on my skin. The water is dark and murky and it feels right. There are lots of salamanders down by the lifeguard station, so I collect them for the kids and keep a hardy stock in rows of aquariums in the nature cabin.

Today my lesson is on the salamander's life cycles. We observe the little animals: me, my campers, and my ghost. "They're the only creature that can metamorphose from aquatic to terrestrial and back to aquatic again. That means they have gills first, then they grow lungs and feet. They live on land for up to eight years, traveling far and wide before switching back to gills, shrinking their legs, and returning to the water as salamanders."

The kids ooh and ahh and my ghost entertains herself by keeping the feathers that are tied to the rafters spinning overhead. She's already heard this spiel half a dozen times today.

I pull a salamander out of the tank and it flops around in my hands. There is something about their eyes. They look blind in their aquatic stage. They creep the kids out a little and I understand why. It's hard to trust something that transforms so completely that it becomes an entirely different animal. They gaze at the salamander tanks with interest, but no one wants to hold them.

After the kids leave I try to eat lunch.

"So how do they do it?" my ghost asks.

I've stoked the firepit outside my tent and I'm grilling a burger. I don't eat a lot these days. My curves are trimmed away, leaving hollows in my cheeks and making caverns of my clavicles.

"Do what?" I take another gulp from my vodka water bottle and squint at her through the smoke.

"How do they change back and forth like that? From newt to salamander."

"Magic," I tell her.

I'm a pretty crap nature specialist even without the alcoholism. Bear didn't hire me for my qualifications. He hired me because I told him about the accident. At least I told him it was why I wanted the job. After she died, I wanted to find something meaningful and fulfilling. I wanted to influence and change lives. I wanted to work at Camp Pispogutt. And I'd kind of meant it at the time. I thought maybe some fresh air would be good for me. A break from routine. A low stress job. As far as Bear was concerned, it was all a part of some grander design. "I don't invest in things, I invest in people," he had said after my speech, clasping me in a hug that explained his name. "There's a reason you found me. Welcome aboard, Regan."

That was the night my ghost showed up, sitting cross-legged in the middle of my bedroom, examining a stack of her old records that her parents had insisted I keep. The Russian nesting dolls I'd given her for one of her birthdays were lined up on my windowsill. Her clothes, which I had packed in giant lawn bags and planned to donate, were strewn around my room in a violent explosion of patterns and colors. They were sad and beautiful haunted garments, mostly impractical and whimsical things that still carried around echoes of her. It was exactly three weeks after she'd died. It was the first step I'd taken away from her.

On my day off, I drive to the closest library that has Wi-Fi. The main office at camp has a computer, but I don't want anyone to see what I'm researching.

"Where are we going?" she asks. Her hair is a puff of silk out the open window. Her profile is perfect. She chain smokes along with me, blowing smoke rings into animal shapes that skate off into the sky. Squirrels, butterflies, salamanders. Her knitting bag is on the passenger-side floor beneath her feet. There are odd shapes bulging through the fabric. I'm almost certain it's where she's keeping the stolen bones. I turn up the music and drive fast along the country roads.

There's no easy way to do this.

At the library, I browse through the books for a while. It's a small town library. I don't expect to find anything I'm looking for, but I grab a few manuals about regional edible plants and wild animals.

"You've already researched that stuff," she comments before wandering off to look in the art section. In life she loved to paint, but it must not have stuck because she's back in a flash, looking over my shoulder at the computer screen as I type "how to get rid of a ghost."

The good thing about becoming a full-blown alcoholic is that I have a water bottle in my purse at the ready. I can get drunk anywhere. I take a long gulp. The warmth that settles over my insides as I read doesn't stop me from noticing that she's crying, but it makes me feel it a little less.

Most of what I find online is unhelpful. I read the signs of supernatural interference: hearing voices, objects appearing or disappearing, electronics turning on and off by themselves, hallucinations, feelings of being watched, animals acting strangely, a sudden urge to overeat, drink, smoke, or do drugs, and nightmares. All understatements. But then, I never doubted I was haunted.

I come across a site with a step-by-step spirit removal process. My ghost reads the steps out loud sarcastically as I scan them:

1) Identify the energy. If your ghost is a loved one who died, realize that it's better for both of you if they go to the Light.

2) Sometimes ghosts are not aware they're dead or being bothersome. Therefore, firmly yet calmly explain out loud that he or she is dead, and it's time to move on to the Light (point upwards). Make sure you are sober and centered during this process or you'll open yourself up to the risk of possession.

3) If the energy does not want to leave, call in God, guides of the Light, and (for tougher cases) archangels, for assistance in guiding the lost soul(s) home.

She's laughing now but I can hear the anger in it.

We leave the library in silence. We walk along the Main Street shops beneath the lacy patterns of tall shade trees, and I don't marvel at the quiet charm of a little New England mountain town. At the hardware store I buy a bucket of red paint and some brushes. The cashier rings me up and gives me a funny look that I'm becoming accustomed to. Something happens to you when you're haunted, and people see it even when they don't recognize what it is.

My ghost is giving me the silent treatment again but I pretend not to notice. My reflection as I pass by storefront windows is alarming. Instead of my standard camp issued clothes, I'm dressed in some faded fluttery garments of hers that I don't recall putting on or packing into my suitcase. I hardly recognize myself in the glass. My last stop in town is the liquor store. I buy a smuggler's ransom worth of cheap vodka.

Back in the car I say, "Listen, it's not because I don't care about you anymore."

She doesn't answer me. Her face is tear-streaked. I want to feel sorry for her, but I know what she wants. She wants my body. She wants my bones.

"It's not right," I say. "You aren't supposed to be here."

"You're so selfish, Regan," she says. Her eyes have turned a solid black. "You owe me. The least you can do is share your life with me. And you won't even do that." She lights a cigarette and blows a stream of smoke right at me. "And if you try any of that new-agey, sage-burning, walking-to-the-light bullshit with me then I really *will* possess you."

I take my time going back to camp. We drive through the mountains, taking in the bright green of new leaves and swirling mist tendrils that soften the forest into someplace magical.

.

By the time we get back to camp, I feel as if I am underwater. The afternoon is a drop of amber, as if time has turned thick and slowed down. It's why I like being drunk so much. I feel burnt and liquid at the same time. Curiously separate from what I'm about to do. I carry the bucket of red paint through the forest and paint two coats on the door of the nature cabin. According to my research, red repels ghosts. It's a place to start anyway.

I paint the inside of the door, too, just in case. Juniper, the filicidal flying squirrel, watches me from her cage. I haul the cage outside, set it on the ground, and open the hinged slider, then go back inside so she can escape on her own terms. The red-eft newts have been captive for over a month now. I carry the terrariums out next to Juniper's empty cage and dump them. I watch their neon skins disappear into the mossy earth. Then the salamanders. Their aquariums are too heavy to lift, so I scoop them up with a net and transfer them to the campfire water bucket. I take the bucket to my campsite and lower it into Beaver Pond.

"What are you doing?" my ghost demands, as the salamanders swim away like gunshots into the water.

I turn my attention to the Russian nesting dolls, ignoring her cries before hurling them into the pond. They bob above the surface for a while, bright smiles painted on their faces, before sinking down beneath the water.

•

Water spiders scurry through the cracks of the floating dock as I walk down to the deepest part of the lake's swimming area. Bay waves from the shore, where he's teaching the Minnow-age swimmers how to tread water. A few of the campers shout my name. I dive into the lake and swim. I breaststroke until I'm out of breath and crampy and Bay is signaling for me to start swimming back.

"Your schoolgirl crush is pathetic," my ghost says. She floats on her back wearing oversized sunglasses. "Do you really think he would like you if he knew the things I know about you?"

I swim underwater, back toward the shore. I can't hear her. I can't see her. It's blessed silence. Just me and the salamanders. I climb up onto the dock.

"You're quite the swimmer," says Bay.

Afternoon lessons with the campers are over and the other lifeguards are closing up the swimming area. I help Bay pick up discarded life jackets and carry them into the boathouse.

I'm still drunk, but hoping the water washed the smell of booze away. Bay doesn't seem to notice.

"Do you have any snorkels?" I ask. "And a mask maybe?"

"Sure," he says. He has a white strip of suntan lotion on his nose. His arms are tanned and muscled. He's vigorously alive. "But you can't see too much in the lake. It's pretty cloudy."

I don't care. I'm imagining hours of uninterrupted silence underwater. He digs out a pair of each and hands them to me. "Just don't go swimming alone," he says. "Bear would kill me. Buddy system. Even for the adults. Come get me if you want to swim."

I nod. My mood's improved a hundred percent.

"Wow," says Bay. "You're smiling."

"Like an idiot," my ghost says.

He smiles back. "What are you doing with the rest of your day off?"

•

We have sex in the boat room. Then in the water. The campers and counselors are at dinner so we have the lakefront to ourselves. Afterwards, I try out my new swimming gear while Bay sits on the dock and watches me dive deep down to the weedy bottom of the lake. Everything is quiet. Mica flecks glimmer in the setting sunlight like fireflies swimming through a silent holy grotto. I hold my breath until my lungs burn before shooting back to the surface for a gulp of air, waving at Bay and diving deep again. My ghost has made herself remarkably scarce. I make a mental note to myself to comment on some of the blogs next time I go to the library. *Ghosts can't bother you when you're snorkeling underwater. Sex with a good-looking lifeguard helps, too.*

"You should change and come down to the bonfire," he

says. It's a weekly camp event that includes all of the campers, instructors, and staff. I know Bear likes to play the bongo drums and has replaced traditional Pispogutt camp songs with some of the ditties the Doshinji monks taught us during training. I have a blurry recollection of them. Songs to fall asleep to. I've never participated in the bonfire before.

"Why not," I say.

That's the moment she chooses to reappear. Her eyes are even blacker now. They are little more than empty holes in her face. It makes the skin on my arms prickle.

"Great," says Bay. "I'll make us some sandwiches. And you should change. Looks like you're getting cold."

"You have to be kidding me!" shouts my ghost. "What are you doing, Regan? First this idiot and now campfire songs with a bunch of brainwashed morons? If you think this is going to cure you, you are so wrong."

I ignore her and strip out of my wet bathing suit, hanging it on a branch to dry. I pull on one of her lacy shirts, jeans that hang on my hip bones now, and a striped hoodie with thumbholes poked in the cuffs. I grab a fresh vodka bottle, smoke a cigarette, perfume myself with bug spray, and pop a mint in my mouth for good measure.

Bay meets me by Big Poppa and we walk to the bonfire spot together. My ghost makes rude comments the whole time. She's determined to ruin the evening. There's a big moon tonight and the stars are bright and low hanging. Fireflies blink on the path around us. The air is fresh with the scent of hemlock trees. She moves above me in the treetops, angrily shaking the leaves. Bay hands me a cheese sandwich and we eat in silence. I wouldn't say I feel happy, exactly. Still, it's the farthest I've felt from alone in a while.

"Do they tell ghost stories at the bonfire?" I ask.

My ghost snorts.

Bay shakes his head. "Bear doesn't like that. As of this year there are no ghosts at Camp Pispogutt."

"Did there used to be?" I ask.

Bay gives me a fiendish smile. "The Goatman. He lived in that abandoned shack down past the nature cabin. Where we keep the tennis nets."

"There's no Goatman," my ghost says.

"What was his story?" I ask.

Bay shrugs. "The usual. Ate little kids. Bad campers. Played pranks. I think he was half goat, but I don't remember why."

"Why would a ghost eat a kid?" she asks.

"How did Bear get rid of him?"

Bay gives me a funny look. "Because he never existed, Regan. You are strange sometimes. Bear just outlawed telling ghost stories. They aren't very Zen, you know?"

My ghost takes offense at this, but we've reached the bonfire. I sit beside Bay. Bear is indeed playing a pair of bongos. The camp music teacher strums a guitar and someone else is playing a triangle. It's amazing that I've been here half the summer and I hardly know anyone besides my ghost.

I vaguely remember the song they're singing, which everyone learned at orientation. The lyrics consist mostly of the words *breathe in, breathe out*. I can't quite bring myself to sing along. Behind me my ghost has made herself comfortable. I tip my head slightly to one side and hear the click-click-click of her knitting needles. She works in tempo with the music. My heart is beating along. The firelight licks at the faces around me. Their words blur and the sounds change. My eyes are heavy-lidded and sleepy. "I feel funny," I tell Bay, but he doesn't seem to hear me.

I tug at his sleeve but he remains impassive.

All of a sudden, my stomach is churning violently. I get to my feet, stagger over to the bushes and begin to heave until I vomit. My lips are slimy and taste like lake water. Beneath me are squirming masses of slick-bellied salamanders.

Everything tilts. The music pounds in my head. I can't see my ghost. I can't find Bay. I can't even make out the faces of the people sitting around the fire. The shapes of the bodies around me twist and contort until they resemble rows of Russian nesting dolls.

I lunge down the hill toward the bathrooms, wiping blood from my mouth. I'm going to be sick again. I have the sudden fear that I'll throw up newts this time. Or tiny chewed up pieces of newborn flying squirrels.

"Hey," says my ghost. She's come after me. "It's okay, Regan, I'm here."

I was stupid to think we could be separated, forever or at all.

I open my mouth to speak but begin vomiting again. I close my eyes so I can't see what it is. I wipe something warm and wet from my chin.

"Come on." She's helping me. We're walking away from the music. Away from the bathrooms and back down toward our campsite. I stop to throw up on Big Poppa. This time I look. Leeches. I fall backward and scramble away, gagging the last few up in long, stretchy pieces.

"It's not real, Regan," she says, trying to still my panic. She looks beautiful in the moonlight, but there is no bottom in those black eyes. They seem to go on forever. When I try to stagger away she is right in front of me again. She's everywhere. I can't escape her.

When we get back to the campsite I collapse in the grass. She hands me my vodka and I gargle with it. I rinse my face and chin. I gulp it down greedily and wait for it to burn away everything that is inside me. I squeeze my eyes shut so I don't have to look at her.

My ghost is knitting. She perches on a rock above me. Stars spin as her needles flash and click and gleam. Something settles over me like a blanket and I feel it choking out the air around me. Soft strands. Silken threads. Vines and seaweed. They wave across my cheek like ripples of water. Then they become sharper. Fireflies, dead butterflies, and bird feathers. The bones are there, woven into some sort of funeral shroud that's curling around my body. I kick and thrash, slicing my skin against sharp pieces of animal skull, struggling to get away from her. In the distance, I can still hear the chanting of Bear's spiritually progressive campfire songs. Somewhere out there are real people who must notice I have disappeared.

"Nobody's coming," she says. "You disappeared a long time ago." Her eyes are giant black caverns now. And I can see myself inside of them. One of us is dead, and the other one is dying.

"Stop fighting," she says. Her voice is gentle now, designed to lull me into forgetting why she's here. But I can't forget. She wants my body. She wants my bones.

Instead, I make for the release of the water. I splash straight in, kicking and swimming as far down as I can go until I'm flat on my belly at the weedy bottom of Beaver Pond. Cool mud. Feathery ferns. The top half of a Russian nesting doll buried in the glittering silt. But my ghost isn't down here. I turn on my back and blow the air out from my lungs, watching the silver bubbles flee towards the surface.

I have always loved the way the surface looks from underneath. It fractures the moonlight and turns fireflies into glowing embers. I try to push the weeds away to see them better. From down here they look like the remains of leftover campfires.

THE BALLAD OF SPARROW FOOT

My name is Sparrow Foot. This is the name given to me by M. Bastien. It is the name I am called by Tatcho, the tiny man who feeds me and cleans my cage.

At each show, M. Bastien hands out little cards printed up with the story of my genesis. He reads them in a booming voice as he introduces me to the waiting crowds.

Behold! Part human, part bird. Sparrow Foot is the last of the winged beasts called the Harpies. Her touch can turn flesh into stone, and her scream can bleach the life from your soul. Though her powers are diluted by human blood, she is capable of pecking her prey to death and tearing through flesh with her sharp claws. Sparrow Foot was found in the abandoned nest of a Mynah bird when she was merely an infant. Upon hatching, she ate her host mother and fellow siblings. She was apprehended by a brave woodcutter, and at once delivered into the custody of M. Bastien's Curious Beastie Bazaar. Since joining our travelling assortment of the magical and the monstrous, Sparrow Foot has learned to speak as a human, and even shows capabilities of rational thought, although she remains a formidable foe, and quite an attraction for the curious observer, the scientific man, and the mystic who is seeking connections to the past. Warning: Don't stand too close to her cage lest she be-spell you with her gilded tongue.

Usually, during a show, M. Bastien has Tatcho poke some slab of meat through the bars of my cage. I tear at it halfheartedly with my one claw while the crowd oohs and aahs. I prefer to eat with my hands, of course, but M. Bastien forbids this. I am to act as a monster. This is what the people come to see.

M. Bastien is not a French aristocrat, as his oiled mustache and shiny top hat may imply. He's a Cajun. Most of his creatures are from the bayou, holding on to some primordial part of their natures. There are pygmies and pinheads, a wolf boy, a web-footed water nymph, and a whole family of lizard people with scaly, prehensile tails. During the shows, M. Bastien turns a *boolye* on us and swings the light from cage to cage. Tatcho prods us with his pole until we rear up and give the audience a thrill.

"Sparrow Foot has more strength in her harpy leg than a boa constrictor attacking its prey," M. Bastien says to the enrapt onlookers. I can hardly see through the blinding spotlight.

It's true. My bird foot is strong. But that's mostly because M. Bastien has put me through rigorous training. Most of the time he forbids me from walking with my human leg. Between shows, I stand for hours with my claw gripping the top of the highest stump in my cage, nodding off from time to time, my whole weight relying on the strength of my feathered limb to keep me upright. My human leg I keep tucked up unobtrusively to my chest. This has resulted in a peculiar engorgement of twisted muscles that make my bird leg more extraordinary. Extraordinary is the word M. Bastien uses when he is introducing me to crowds. *Extraordinary. Magnificent. Amazing. Rare.* But the words don't seem to mean what they are supposed to mean. Usually the crowds jostle for a better view and yell out rude comments. I'm used to it.

During intermissions M. Bastien's trained macaque, Cecil, cycles around on a miniature bicycle wearing a smoking jacket and fedora. He does outrageous tricks, like juggling bananas as he pedals, or performing handstands on his seat. After intermission the lights dim and the mood becomes somber. M. Bastien always saves the big numbers for last. The final act is Percival, the wolf boy. Percival isn't as scary as he sounds. He lives in the cage next to mine and he's my best friend here. He's less of a wolf and more of a boy with a lot of hair. That doesn't stop crowds from going wild over him.

Minette, the web-footed water nymph, is a more recent acquisition. She still blushes deep green when the spotlight swings her way. M. Bastien dresses her in wispy concoctions of leafy material. She wears a headdress of waterweeds and wilted swamp orchids. The sorrow in her eyes has seeped down to make dark hollows in her face.

"Her lovely looks are only a ruse," M. Bastien says. "Really she's one of the most cunning beasts in the bayou. Jeune fille. If she happens to catch you too close to the water's edge, prepare to curse your immortal soul by joining her graveyard below the water." Minette arrived last week. She was put in a cage on the other side of Percival. It's the most exciting thing that's happened around here in a while, although she refuses to speak to anyone and stays curled up in a ball in the corner.

Only when Tatcho comes to poke his stick through the bars of her cage does she come to life, hissing wildly and flashing her teeth.

•

Lots of people look at me from afar, but none get too close. I'm not pretty enough to change my "monster" status to "exotic." I'm knotted and mottled. The color of moss and dead wood. My feathers don't form glorious aerial constructions, but sprout unevenly over my body. I have two fleshy, unformed nubs on my back in place of wings. My throat is thick and my eyes are so large and yellow that people jump when I blink. In truth, I don't look much like any sparrow I've ever seen.

I'm surprised when the young man with the sandy hair starts hanging around my cage.

"I'm Jacob," he says. "Do you mind if I sketch you?"

I nod. Meanwhile, a handful of overly perfumed middle-aged women are flirting with Percival, who is dutifully trying to be suave and dangerous at the same time.

Jacob pulls out a leather notebook and pencil and gets to work while I flap about uncomfortably. I wonder what part of me he's drawing. He's looking at my bird foot. His eyes are memorizing the patterns of my feathers. I am still as a stone as he studies the nubs where my wings should be.

"What's your name?" he asks.

"Sparrow Foot," I say. It comes out sounding breathy and I blush beneath my feathers.

Jacob pauses at his sketching and his eyes latch on to mine. "I mean your real name. The name your parents gave you?"

"Sparrow Foot *is* my real name. I have no parents."

The look on Jacob's face is pure pity. I can't stand it. No one should ever look at a monster this way. Sometimes I deal with things by closing my eyes and blending into my perch. If I tilt my head up toward the sky my tangled hair makes me look like a mossy extension of the branch. That's how I deal with the pity on Jacob's face, and when I open my eyes again he is gone.

"Well, well," Percival teases later. "Someone's finally got a suitor."

I roll one big, yellow eye at him and act cool. "We can't all have your gift of overactive pheromone excretion," I say as he sucks on a chocolate strawberry that had been pushed between the bars of his cage by one of his middle-aged doters.

·

Jacob comes every day that week and we forge an awkward friendship that consists mostly of him sketching me and taking notes. He says he's a birder. I have no idea what that is.

"I look for birds," he explains. "All over the world." He motions to the binoculars hanging around his neck. "The rarer the better."

"What do you do with them?" I ask and he laughs.

"Nothing. Just watch. Listen. Take notes."

"Sounds like an awfully fancy hobby," I tell him.

He gives me a shiny necklace that I bury in the dirt. I've got some nickels hoarded away beneath the soil, along with shiny buttons purloined from M. Bastien's top coat.

In the back of my throat I feel a funny tickle. When I look at Jacob, the tickle slides further down into my chest and begins to pulse. It's a distant yet familiar feeling. I want to tell him something I have no words for.

·

Among the monsters things are getting tense. There's more creeping and slinking than usual. I think it's because of the water nymph. She exudes some quality that seems to make all of the warm—and even cold—blooded males want to protect her. She is frail to the point of sharpness. Her shoulders jut out at right angles. Tatcho places a small pool of water in her cage each morning. After the first few rebellious days of splashing Tatcho and M. Bastien whenever they walk past, she finally gives in and takes to wetting her skin constantly. This makes her complexion dewy. A fact that has not gone unnoticed by Percival.

"Stare any harder and you'll melt the bars," I tell him.

He scowls at me. Maybe. With his surplus of facial hair it's really difficult to make out a discernible expression. "I've never seen a nymph before," he says.

There's something about Percival. Maybe it's because he's my only friend here. Or maybe it's the sheer excess of male hormones he produces, but it makes me check my harpy tongue. I don't point out that none of us are what we seem. Instead I groom my patchy plumage and suffer the pangs of jealousy silently. Percival has been here longer than I have. He's been the wolf boy most of his life. I have only been Sparrow Foot for a few years.

•

Before I joined the Beastie Bazaar, M. Bastien bought me from a bayou witch who used to pass me off as a rougaroux to keep superstitious Cajuns away. Rougaroux are the most cursed beasts in the bayou. They're usually wolves and crocodiles, but any kind of shapeshifting beast will do. Until M. Bastien bought me I always believed that I *was* a rougaroux. Many a full moon I sat in eager anticipation, though I never once shifted.

"Lots of rougaroux don't change until after their first kill," the witch told me, when I got discouraged. "And sometimes it comes with womanhood." When I pressed her for details she got surly. "You've got a bird claw for a foot. What else do you need to know?"

Sometimes, mostly at night, when the bullfrogs were deep harrumphing and the Louisiana moon hung off the naked branches of cypress trees, I felt something like an itch all the way deep down in my soul. I waited for my skin to peel away and my body to become all bird, but it never happened. I stayed patchy and half formed, no matter how I urged my tiny wing nubs to grow, or how many animals I killed for dinner.

Although she wasn't particularly maternal, I lived a substantially better life in the witch's stilt shack. I had some freedom at least. She taught me how to read and write and I spent my days helping her collect ingredients and boil potions and stews. I took to studying her maps at night while she slept, and memorizing the names of distant lands. I may be the only monster in the Bazaar who knows every country from Afghanistan to Zimbabwe.

Then one day M. Bastien showed up to collect on a debt and haggled her into selling me. Imagine my surprise to find out that I was no rougaroux at all. I was a harpy. A whole different kind of monster. The very last of my kind, according to him.

"Such a shame," he said, curling one end of his oiled mustache around his finger as we drove away in his carriage, leaving the bayou witch and the little shack behind us. "A fine specimen like you just collecting dust as if you were *ordinary*." The way he said "ordinary" made it sound like a terrible quality. "You were made to be worshipped! You were made to be in the spotlight and gazed upon."

For the first time, I looked down at my bird's leg with something akin to pride. Fireflies winked with hope in the deep, wet night around us. Up ahead I could see the colorful lights of the traveling caravans that made up the Curious Beasties Bazaar. I imagined creatures of all kinds coming out to greet me as we arrived. Future friends. Kindred spirits. We passed the bonfires, the performers, and the smell of gumbo. M. Bastien took me straight to a large area fenced in with barbwire. Inside were dozens of cages in which dull eyes reflected his lantern's glow. He led me to an empty cage full of criss-crossing branches. There was a tiny nest high up in one corner, and the floor was padded with thick bunches of Spanish moss hopping with fleas and lice.

"This is your new home," M. Bastien said, ushering me inside and turning a key in the lock behind me. "*Bon soir*, Sparrow Foot."

A hirsute boy groomed himself in the cage beside mine. He peered at me through glossy waves of hair, his double rows of pointed teeth gleaming bright in the night. "Welcome," he said. "And get used to holding your nose. There was a skunk ape in there before you."

That first night, I cried myself to sleep, homesick for my bed and the familiar sound of water lapping at the shore. I was around nine years old, I think.

•

As the days pass, Minette unsuccessfully campaigns to win her freedom. She tries sweet talking Tatcho, but the little man barely understands a word of English or French, aside from M. Bastien's brusque commands. He doesn't seem affected by her charms. He wears a gris-gris cross around his neck that he uses to ward her off. She tries her hardest to be seductive, but Tatcho grimaces at her bare breasts and holds up his cross.

"*Pischouette!*" she yells at him in frustration. "*Fils de putain!*"

Tatcho swigs tequila from a flask on his belt and mumbles to himself in Spanish. He pretends his fingers are guns and points them in the air, rapid-firing invisible bullets.

Percival and I watch the exchange quietly. Minette is looking for things to fling from her cage. "*Merde!*" she shouts. "*Tcheue poule!*" Percival looks to me to translate. I shrug. I may be part harpy but I don't repeat things like that.

Then Minette chucks her chamber pot, clipping Tatcho mid-swig. He howls and hops around. The cages on the other side of Minette belong to the family of lizard people and, in no time at all, they've joined the revolt. They let loose a hail of sticks and mud and chamber pot contents of their own. I watch Percival struggle against his bestial nature to remain uninvolved. He considers himself more civilized than most of the creatures here. Still, the combined effect of the spreading chaos and the nymph's powers of seduction have his hair standing on end and his breathing shallow.

This is my first insurrection. I find myself stunned into inaction and take up my defensive posture. With my chin pushed up and my back straight, I blend right in with the stump and wait.

Within moments whips crack the air. M. Bastien and two of his henchmen squelch the rebellion with a few practiced blows. Tatcho hovers behind the bigger men. "Now," M. Bastien says in a dulcet tone. "Who is behind this, hmm? I can flog you all or I can flog the creature responsible. Which will it be?"

Minette cowers in one corner of her cage.

The lizard people sit in unified silence.

After a moment, to my surprise, Percival stands forward.

"What are you doing?" I hiss. He's wearing an expression so noble I want to throw something at him. There is no glory in facing M. Bastien's punishments.

•

Once we had a mermaid girl whose unformed legs were fused together in the shape of a tail. She didn't look much like the mermaids of legend. She was rather husky, with a wide moon-shaped face and a thick unibrow. She couldn't breathe underwater so she just paddled around in her giant tank, making her way along the edges and sometimes hauling herself over the sides to sunbathe. She wasn't locked away like the rest of us, because she couldn't get far on her own outside of the water. The best she could do was flop about. She tried to make a game out of tossing fallen berries from the Chinaball trees back and forth with the rest of us. Aside from the Pinheads, most of the other monsters ignored her.

But mermaid girl had moxie. She was always saying inspirational things to herself as she paddled along. Words of encouragement and phrases like, "I can do anything I put my mind to, I just have to remember to try extra hard," and "God broadens the back to bear the burden." Her attitude bewildered the monsters, so she didn't make a lot of friends. Still, it was hard not to be charmed by her inexplicably sunny disposition.

One moonless night mermaid girl escaped. It took a while for M. Bastien to put together how she'd done it. Somehow she'd concocted a set of wheels to strap her tail into by using a plank of wood and various disassembled parts from the miniature bicycle that Cecil rode during intermissions. The monkey was furious and M. Bastien even more so. But by the time the sun came up, mermaid girl was long gone, just a set of dusty tire tracks left in the earth. That was the first time I remember feeling hope.

A few days later M. Bastien returned with mermaid girl in tow. He made a new tank for her. This one had a lid and no air inside of it. In order to breathe, she relied on a single hose that poked down through the top of the tank. This kept her silent and immobile. It was terrible to see her floating around through the clear glass like that. Her eyes turned pale and cloudy, her skin puffy and bloated. Her fleshy tail flapped about helplessly. She didn't last long like that. She took ill and died, and M. Bastien had her taxidermied and retired to the hall of monsters.

We, all of us, felt terrible about mermaid girl. She taught me one of my first and most important lessons in the Beastie Bazaar: caring about other monsters comes at a terrible price. Bravery is a useless trait. And even the most wild and fearless creature has their spirit broken sooner rather than later here.

Which is why Percival's action is so horrifying. I feel a wave of fury for the water nymph as M. Bastien and his henchmen remove Percival from his cage and haul him off toward the main camp. The nymph barely seems to notice.

"You horrible thing!" I yell at her. She's placing cold compresses on her face. "What have you done?"

She gives me a pouty look of incomprehension. "It is not my fault," she says, in a thick French accent. "He volunteered."

"You don't know what they'll do to him," I say.

Minette watches me now, curiously. "Wolf boy is your *paramour*?"

I shake my head, but I can't stop the tears from coming. At first it's tears, then racking sobs that knock me off my perch.

I lie huddled in a pile of moss, imagining Percival tortured or taxidermied. It's terrible. Monsters aren't supposed to cry.

The nymph positions herself on the side of her cage that's closest to mine. "Here," she says, wetting some leaves and tying them into a poultice. She throws them to me through the bars of Percival's empty cell. "Put these on your face," she says, miming how to arrange them. "These will soothe you. There is nothing you can do for him tonight, Sparrow Foot. Get some rest and maybe he will be back tomorrow."

•

The next morning Percival's cage is still empty, but Jacob comes to see me. I feel hollow from all the crying. He has his leather notebook and another package, too. It's bigger and looks heavy.

"You don't look well," he says, examining me carefully. "Are you okay?"

I ignore him and concentrate on blending into my perch. I am not okay. I am trying to figure out how to draw on the strength of my harpy ancestors to overthrow this Beastie Bazaar and rescue Percival.

Jacob sits down beside my cage and loosens the knot in the scarf around his neck. As always, he is healthy and wholesome. Sandy blond hair. Inquisitive grey eyes. "I was hoping we could talk today," he says.

I think of refusing, but just then Tatcho walks by and clanks on the bars of my cage with a stick. I give him a hot yellow glare and he yells something at me in Spanish.

"Who's that?" asks Jacob.

"Our beastkeeper," I say. "He feeds us."

I watch his Adam's apple bob up and down as he writes this in his little notebook. "What do you like to eat?"

It's a question that only someone who hasn't been imprisoned would ask. I say, "I eat what I'm given."

Jacob takes a jar out of his pocket. He untwists the top of it and shakes a couple of nuts into his palm. "Do you like cashews? Here."

"I don't think of food in terms of 'like.'"

He holds the nuts close to the cage. Guests are not supposed to feed the monsters but they do. Jacob watches my arm extend toward him and I'm surprised at how filthy it is compared to his own soft white skin. My fingernails are hideously sharp and black. I grab the whole jar and shake the contents into my mouth. The nuts are delicious. Buttery and something else. They taste like old memories.

Jacob laughs a clean, strong laugh—nothing like the laughter of men that I am used to. The sound of it warms my belly.

"You like them," he says, "I'll bring you some more next time."

I settle into my still-as-a-stone position, although inside my heart beats a funny rhythm. I reward Jacob's kindness by sitting with my bird leg displayed in full prominence.

"I brought you something else today," he says, and I squeeze one eye open a slit to see him push a shiny package between the bars of my cage and under a clump of moss with the toe of his clean loafers. "I think you'll like it."

I shudder slightly with excitement, but if Jacob notices he is too polite to mention it.

"I'm going to draw you now, if that's okay." I maintain my posture, despite that deep pulse, which is becoming more like a thrum in my chest. It feels like rubber bands stretched to snapping. While he draws, Jacob tells me about cashew nuts. "In Brazil they are called *marañón*," he says. "The nut grows from the end of a cashew apple. They are a fruit on top of a fruit. The outsides are poison until they are roasted and shelled. During the war, cashews were used to sabotage German vehicles by pouring their oil into the crankcases of engines. They took out entire battalions. Hard to believe one little nut can do all of that, huh?"

I act as if I'm not listening because I'm unsure of how to respond. Under the steamy Louisiana sun and with the rich mellow tones of Jacob's voice, making conversation as he sketches, the tightness in my chest relaxes and I am suddenly exhausted. My lids grow heavy and close on the image of Jacob bent over his notebook, his face serious with concentration.

·

When I wake up, Jacob is gone and Tatcho is walking around on a pair of stilts, lighting colored lanterns in the branches of the Chinaball trees. I hoard my jar of cashews under a pile of twigs. The package I move up to my nest. I nearly shred the wrapping in my eagerness to see what's inside.

It's a book. *The Big Book of the Birds of the World.* Inside are colorful pictures and drawings of all varieties of amazing and majestic birds. Most of them I've never seen before. Some have long necks, brilliant plumage, and feathers like silken tassels. Beautiful things from all over the world. Relatives of mine. The vivid shades and dramatic designs make my blood pump. I let out a few involuntary warbling noises as I turn the pages carefully.

"*Ooo lala,*" Minette says as she prepares for the evening show. "Love is in the air, *oui*, Sparrow Foot?"

I'm still irked with her for getting Percival taken away. I carefully cover the book with moss so she can't see it.

"Come here," she says seductively. "Take a beauty lesson. You will never hold the attention of your visitor man with *cheveux* like a water buffalo's ass."

My hair is a mess of tangled dreadlocks that fall down my back. Hers is luxurious and long, with lilies and green turtle shells woven into the braids. I hop down closer where I can see her just as a comb and mirror come whizzing through the bars of my cage.

Minette coaches me through the painstaking process of detangling the clumps of my hair. She claps her hands and yells at Tatcho for more water. "*Boisson!*" she shouts. "*Merde!*" Her snarls keep him hotfooting between our two cages with buckets of water. She has a stash of Chinaballs that the lizard people have collected for her. She hurls them at Tatcho when he isn't looking. Her aim is impeccable.

I have not bathed in a long time. The dirt makes it easier to blend in here. Under Minette's tutelage, I do my best to clean myself, but it still feels slightly wrong. Everything in my nature tells me to stay hidden. I think of all of those birds in my bird book, each one reveling in their distinct differences until I feel bold again.

"Minette," I say as I scrub at my nails. "What's your family like?"

She rolls her eyes. "*Mamere* was a whore. *Bon rienne.*" She throws herself down on a pile of moss and pulls at the petals of a water lily. "Who needs family? I only care about lovers. Besides, I have my own pond with loblolly pines and dancing cypress." She smiles, revealing teeth carved into fine points. "I go back there after I get out of this piss-hole of a freak show."

•

By the time Tatcho swings the *boolye* on us and M. Bastien begins the show, I have transformed. I feel naked before the crowd, but I stand up straight on my bird leg and face the audience rather than try to blend into my surroundings.

Gasps swirl around me from the surprised crowd. My hair falls down in shining coils laced with feathers I've gathered from the bottom of my cage. Minette helped me fashion some into a crown and even glued some longer ones to my eyelashes for dramatic effect. It doesn't make me beautiful, but it does make me remarkable.

Although I can't see the audience, M. Bastien looks annoyed. He touches my chin with the tip of his cane and tilts my head back and forth until I quiver. This seems to satisfy him and he moves along to the next monster.

Percival is still missing. His cage has been left behind in the dark. When it's Minette's turn, she flounces about in her translucent garments, whipping the crowd into a fine frenzy. She pouts and blows kisses until the men roar.

After the show we are returned to our containment area and Percival's cage is missing altogether. Tatcho and the beastkeepers place my cage directly beside Minette's. She sees the alarmed expression on my face as I take in our new arrangements. "*Non. Non,*" she says forcefully. "It will do no good to cry."

"This is your fault," I say. I pound on the bars of my cage until Tatcho smacks me with a plank of wood.

There is a terrible welling deep inside me. My lungs fill and my throat pulses with something foreign, something that feels powerful and alive. If I were really a harpy, I could do something to save Percival. If I were really a rougaroux, I could curse M. Bastien and Tatcho and anyone who got in my way.

"We need to stick together," Minette is saying, but I don't want any more of her advice. I retreat to my nest and settle myself around *The Big Book of Birds*. My mind whirls as I turn the pages. I devour the information greedily, trying not to think of my only friend being tortured and maimed. Or even worse... lost to me forever.

Although nothing makes me forget about Percival, there are all sorts of birds to learn about. King-fishers, Dabbling ducks, Button-quills, Flamingos, Blue-tits, Sunbirds, Lorikeets, Great Frigates, and Masked Boobies. I am dizzy with the sheer number of them. I spend most of the night perched over the pages, nodding off only when the sun begins to climb the sky. Even then, my dreams are filled with all variations of feathers, beaks, plumage, and scales.

•

In the morning, there are some overripe bananas and a bruised orange on the floor of my cage, courtesy of Tatcho. I cover my book and hop down for breakfast.

Minette splashes about her pool noisily. From the sound of her tra-la-la-ing you wouldn't know that she's locked up against her will.

"Sparrow Foot," she calls. "*Venir*! We need to talk before the visitors arrive." She's taken on quite a commandeering presence in the short time she's been here. I watch as she bathes herself languidly. "I am thinking about something. And I know you are thinking about it too," she says.

"What?" I'm still angry with her, shared beauty regimen aside.

"Escape." The word slides out of her mouth in a whisper and I freeze. There's no one close enough to hear, but it still makes me uncomfortable.

"*I* am thinking of rescuing my friend," I say.

Minette shrugs. "It is the same. You can't do one without the other. We must work together. You're the only other one with half a brain in here."

93

But there is no time for plotting. Today the visitors are nearly bursting at the gates. I suspect this is because of the performance Minette put on the night before. Sure enough, a steady stream of men winds around the other cages and stop outside Minette's. Shoulder to shoulder, they make a barrier that I can't see past. Minette coos and giggles flirtatiously. I hope that it's a part of her escape plan.

I return to my nest and bury myself in my book again. Learn a little more about myself. I learn most birds have four chambered hearts, hollow bones, and a posterior air sac good for cycling oxygen in and out of the lungs. The hollow bones are especially necessary for both singing and for flying.

Jacob arrives in the early afternoon, just when I'm starting to feel sleepy. My studies have convinced me I am most likely nocturnal.

"Hello," he says. "Your hair looks nice."

I nod at him. I can't bring myself to mention the book. It feels like too big of a thing between us.

"I brought you something new to try." He pulls a pouch out of his pocket and hands it to me. Our fingers touch for a moment between the bars. I'm glad Minette made me clean myself. This time our skin looks similar except for the smattering of downy feathers running up my arm.

"What's inside?"

He grins. "Thimbleberries. Try one. I think you'll like them."

The thimbleberries are small and sweet. If I close my eyes I can almost taste the place where they came from.

"Do you feel like talking today?" Jacob asks.

I nod.

He studies me for a while and then pulls out his notebook. "Where did you live before you came here?"

"With a witch," I tell him. "In a stilt house on the bayou."

"There was no woodcutter," he says.

It takes me a moment to remember the words printed on my card. "No."

He sketches me silently for a while and then asks, "Do you ever sing?"

"No," I say. "Never." I never learned how to sing. I can sort of hum, like a human. "Sometimes I feel a pressure in my lungs," I tell him.

He smiles. "And you've never tried to let it out? You're lucky it hasn't killed you yet."

I stare at his kind face and clear grey eyes. "I'm going to escape," I say. "I have to rescue a friend."

My words surprise me, but he just nods and asks, "Can I do anything to help?"

I haven't thought that far along. Minette would have a thousand ideas, but I have none.

He sketches me a while longer and then gets to his feet. "Try looking in the book," he says. "Look under Brazilian passerines."

My lungs throb with pressure. I want to fling myself at the cage and thank him for everything. No one has ever been so kind to me. But I'm so emotional I go into camouflage mode without thinking. Back straight. Chin up. Still as a stone.

"Goodbye, Sparrow Foot," he says.

I crack an eye open to watch him walk away.

•

While Minette is fending off the last of her suitors, I am reading all about Brazilian passerines. Most simply, they are birds with grasping toes. There are many different species, but only one with yellow eyes and feathers like tree bark: the

Great Potoo, a rare bird with a wide, short beak and cryptic plumage that blends perfectly with its surroundings. They are related to Nightjars and Frogmouths, though they alone have the abnormally large yellow eyes and uncanny ability to turn into tree stumps. They bury shiny objects and knickknacks. More than anything else, Great Potoos are known for intense loyalty and the magnificence of their haunting calls. It does not surprise me to discover that cashews and thimbleberries are among their favorite foods.

I read on until I come to the end, and then I read it all again, studying the familiar pictures beside the descriptions. My heart is thudding, throat thick, a pressure building inside me. My chest swells with something like pride or bravery.

"Sparrow Foot," Minette calls. Her cage is strewn with flowers from admirers. "Come here!" In a hushed tone, she tells me that one of her lovestruck fans has promised to try to steal the keys from Tatcho as he works. We both agree that the best chance for success is during the show itself, where we will be able to cause instant chaos. Minette will set herself free, then unlock my cage. I will free all of the other monsters, and of course, find Percival amidst the confusion. If we cause some kind of frenzied stampede, M. Bastien will have a hard time corralling all of us. We don't tell the other monsters our plans. We trust they'll follow our lead.

•

The show starts. M. Bastien regales the crowd with his shiny top hat and swinging cane. The light glares down on me. I rear up and open my eyes wide as the familiar words echo around me: *Behold! Part human, part bird. Sparrow Foot is the last of the winged beasts called the Harpies…*

Next are the Pinheads. Next *should be* the Pinheads. Instead, the show skips ahead to Minette, catching us off guard. But the nymph recovers quickly, slipping easily into her seductress act. She gets the crowd worked up and cheering rowdily. Catcalls shriek through the air, but the energy is off. Something is wrong. I can feel it. She curtseys for the crowd and the spotlight swings again.

M. Bastien wheels a platform to the center of the stage. On the platform is a hulking shape, bent on one knee, impossible to see clearly in the flashing lights, but I know immediately that it is Percival.

"And now," M. Bastien says to the roll of the drums. "Perhaps the most feared beast of them all. Not content to sate his hunger on animals alone, this monster recently escaped his confines and was caught in the bayou feasting on the fresh corpse of a dead child. Behold, in all of his horrible glory... Percival the Wolf Boy!"

The audience shrieks as the lights swing on Percival, who is shackled to the platform with iron chains. His carefully coiffed hair is tangled and matted with blood. His eyes are bloodied and swollen and one of his legs is clearly broken. M. Bastien raises his whip and cracks it against Percival's flayed skin. Percival howls and arches his back, splattering the crowd with his blood. It's the most terrifying thing I have ever seen. The crowd erupts in bloodthirsty cheers and I worry that they might rush the stage before I can get to Percival. Even the nymph is caught off guard by the spectacle.

"Minette," I yell, and nearly choke as a strange gurgle fills my throat. At the sound of my voice she snaps back into action, quickly gathering the Chinaballs and getting into place. There is a strange lightness taking over my body. The gurgle is coming from my lungs, a pressure deep inside my belly, as if it is waiting to erupt.

•

It is written in *The Big Book of Birds of the World* that the cry of a Great Potoo can make an entire village weep for months. I am not a Great Potoo. I may resemble one. I may wear their feather patterns and share their blood, but I am something else entirely. I am Sparrow Foot. Not a witch's rougaroux or a huckster's harpy. I am a monster in my own right. When the battle cry finally lets loose from my throat, the entire bayou stands at attention.

Minette throws a Chinaball and shatters the *boolye*. The spotlight falls from Percival's ragged shoulders and we're all plunged into sudden blackness. Monsters bellow their rage, their sorrow, their sadness, but it disappears in the dark.

My lungs suck air until it feels as if the entire world will shatter. Humans grasp at their throats for breath. Crumpled Beastie Bazaar tickets and dollar bills form miniature cyclones in the swirling air. Spanish moss pirouettes and holds tight to keep from being sucked out of the trees. The air sparkles before me. I am the one who has swallowed up the night. I feel it spreading to the insides of my hollow bones. All of it. Expanding until it has pushed my wings out through my shoulders and expanding still until my posterior air sacs are filled and I am taught as a drum. Then I exhale.

The top of the tent lifts off as if by a rogue wind, exposing the tableau to the sky. The bayou is alive with flying creatures. As my lungs empty there are birds everywhere. Feathers flapping against skin. Claws scratching bloody trails through flesh.

Although the Great Potoo is found only in Brazil, it has relatives everywhere. Passerines are the most common genus of bird here in the bayou, and their lineages can all be traced back to one beginning. I am surrounded by my subjects. Nightjars, tawny frogmouths, goatsuckers, lyre birds, butcher birds, berrypickers, wattle eyes, whippoorwills, and cuckoo shrikes. They all come to my call.

I feel the timpanic membranes in my chest go to work in a circular motion. My song doesn't stop when I breathe. It continues on and on forever. The air is filled with flapping. Long-beaked species like the honeyeaters and the bristle birds make short work of the locked cages, while the bigger birds attack the beastkeepers and wreak havoc upon the humans.

As soon as my cage is opened, I fly to the platform where Percival is shackled. My wings are spectacular, my body no longer clunky. M. Bastien lies on his back like a crab, a few feet away, holding his whip in front of him like a weapon. I forget that he's blind in the dark.

"Percival," I say. He's only semi-conscious. There's a flurry of movement at his wrists and ankles and the shackles fall away. "Come on," I say, lifting him to my shoulder, his blood smearing my chest.

The screams and hisses and sounds of tails slithering tells me the other monsters are free as well. I catch glimpses of scaled skin and swishing tails. Minette stands atop an overturned bleacher clutching an armful of Chinaballs. Her pointy teeth are bared but her skin is white with fear.

"Come on," I say, pulling her down beside me. She can't see much, but she knows my voice. She recognizes Percival's limp form over my shoulder and takes a moment to marvel at my wings. Then we are running through the wreckage and into the forest faster than the wind. All around us the bayou shudders and shakes with the echo of my cry. Chinaballs fall and raindrops shake loose from the sky. My wings are a new force. With the added weight of Percival and Minette it takes a few false starts before I am fully off the ground. But once I'm in the air, it's as if I've had these wings forever. I fly until the earth quiets and the night becomes calm around us. Minette whispers directions into my ear.

•

Minette's pond is small and fragrant, covered in water lilies and sheltered by a ring of loblolly trees. I lay Percival down in the grass and Minette sets to gathering herbs and making poultices while I wash the blood from his matted fur. It's hard to tell how deep the wounds are, but Minette takes over like a trained healer. Soon, he's cleaned and bandaged and sedated with moonshine.

"*Mais, jamais d'la vie!*" says Minette as we finally sit back and look at each other. Her frail features are streaked and smeared with blood. She reaches out a hand to touch my wings.

We sit side by side in the moonlight for a while. Then we bathe together in her pond. I want to ask if there are really watery graves of her drowned lovers at the bottom, but in the silver light Minette looks like a young girl. I'm too tired to believe in monsters any longer. Besides, she's a gracious host. She makes a bed for Percival out of soft bulrushes and finds me a stump the exact color of my feathers. My new wings close around me like a blanket and I am asleep before the sun comes up.

An Addendum to The Big Book of Birds of the World

by Jacob R. Wright

There is only one time in history that a Great Potoo has used its song to rally friends and conquer enemies, although the event in question is sparsely documented. It is most commonly known as "The Ballad of Sparrow Foot," and though the creature in question was possibly not a bird and definitely not a sparrow, she displayed many of the peculiar characteristics of the Potoo. She had a six-foot wingspan and eyes like golden platters. Like the Potoo, Sparrow Foot was capable of uncanny camouflaging techniques and the circular singing made possible by multi-timpanic air chambers. Her vocal projection carried across several miles and was even measured afterwards in a study of ground tremors. Her song can still be heard in the bayous of Louisiana, echoing through the marshes and carrying across lonely, wild, moon-filled nights.

WHEN THE WATER WITCHES COME DANCING FOR THEIR SUPPER

The Rusalki wait outside my window every night. White lips, grotesque smiles, green hair streaming with silver fish and lily pads. It's like being in an aquarium. The Rusalki point and jeer through the glass. They tap on the frosted panes with icicle fingernails. *Pretty little thing*, they whisper, *come outside so we can see you better*. I pull a quilt over my face, though I still hear them singing, *We choose you*, over and over. Their voices sound like creaking lake ice.

"Nonsense," says Babci, as we drink our morning tea and look out at the powdered white landscape. Babci is from the old world. She resembles a withered parsnip. She is rooted to her surroundings in a way I can't quite understand. Her feet are heavy. Her skirts are voluminous. Even her white hair grows thick and long, as if determined to plant itself into the ground.

"Silly superstitions," she says, as she ties red yarn around my wrists. This is our morning ritual. She puts salt in my shoes and sticks a saltshaker in my backpack as an extra precaution. Red keeps the Rusalki away. Salt melts ice, and the Rusalki are made from ice and anger.

Before school, we play Scrabble and, when it's my turn, I spell out a vulgar word in Polish.

"Hannah!" she exclaims. "What on earth has gotten into you?"

I shrug. It's the Rusalki telling me what to do, but if I tell her this she will say I'm being absurd, and tie red ribbons in my hair.

"Your parents would be turning in their graves to see you acting out like this," she says.

But my parents have no graves. My mother is a Rusalka. Babci knows this. It's why she takes extra care to make me not believe in them. It's why the water witches want me. I begin to remind her of this but Babci stops me. *Pop. Pop.* Her knuckles crack, ending the conversation. Her arthritis is especially bad in cold weather. She can no longer remove her wedding ring, no matter how much butter or grease we apply. Instead she keeps it wrapped in white athletic tape and gauze, fearing rogue thieves will chop off her finger for the diamonds.

•

When new snow falls, the Rusalki sing songs to the frozen moon. It sounds something like stars and ice rubbing up against each other, terrible and beautiful all at once. When this happens, the villagers stuff cloth beneath the doors and pull heavy drapes across the windows.

Our village is made up of homespun Polish immigrants. The air is thick with the accents of the old-timers here. Their stories escape from brick chimneys, swirled with scotch, cabbage soup, and wood smoke.

Babci is one of them. Her voice is graveled with hardship. Despite her objection to my belief in the Rusalki, she's as superstitious as they come. In our house, we always close the lids to the toilets. We throw herbs on the fire in the evenings so Babci can watch the swirls of smoke and try to make sense out of what they tell her. She times my showers (neither one of us take baths) and wipes all the drains in the house clean of any drops of water. In front of our house is a holly tree with crimson berries that protect us from the dead water witches. That's what Babci believes.

The more Babci insists the Rusalki aren't there, the more I feel drawn to them. They are terrible in the wintertime. They shriek and wail and their eyes glow silver and green in the moonlight. If my mother comes to my window, I wouldn't know it. She wouldn't resemble any picture Babci's ever shown me. She's been dead under the water for nearly sixteen years. These scaly creatures are her sisters. They come on her behalf, singing all night, and in the mornings silver fish and seaweed decorate the snow outside my bedroom window. Babci scoops them up with a shovel and burns them in a fire-pit outside.

Inside she surrounds us with clutter and color, and locks the windows shut every night. Our house is claustrophobic and full of junk. Silk flowers, tea sets, microscopes, baskets of Pysanky eggs, straw crosses, and knitted toilet paper cozies with dolls' heads on them. Babci puts labels on the bottom of everything to designate who will receive her treasures when she dies. Though most of the stuff will go to me, there are several items that still have my mother's name written on them. How do you pass your treasure along to a ghost, I want to know?

It's impossible for Babci to admit the Rusalki are trying to steal me. Then she would have to acknowledge what happened to her own daughter. My mother disgraced Babci by getting pregnant out of wedlock. I don't know who my father was, but Babci likes to say he was a soldier who died in a war. She says my mother drowned not long after I was born, that she was swimming in the lake and got tangled in weeds. It seems as unlikely to me as any Babci story. Babci *says* she sent my mother's body back to Poland so she could rest in the place she came from, but I don't believe her. I think she is still hidden somewhere under the water. Why else would the water witches come? Whatever happened to my mother's body, her soul is still here.

•

We continue to play Scrabble when I return from school. I try to stop my swearing, but the urges are even stronger and, despite myself, I spell out *Suka. Szmata. Kurwa.* And then my mother's name. *Zofia.* Until finally Babci swipes the tiles off the board and into the box. I feel terrible, but it's as if someone else is controlling my hands. She tries teaching me pinochle, but her concentration is shot. The long nights are getting shorter. When winter ends, the lake in the forest will thaw and the Rusalki will become more powerful. In June they are at their strongest. All of the villagers stay away from the lake in June. June is when my mother died.

"I think we should send you away," says Babci. I'm winning at pinochle, but that just shows how little she's paying attention to the game. The wind howls outside and blows rain onto the window glass.

"I'm not leaving," I say. "Where would I go? Besides, this is my home."

"I don't know," she says. "But something has to be done." *Pop. Pop. Pop.* Babci carefully unhinges her fingers and takes my hand in hers, which is swollen and hard. "Maybe we can send you away to another school," she says.

I smile politely to try to ease her distress. We both know she doesn't have any money.

She pulls her hands away and hops up from our game. She

grabs a pail of salt from the kitchen and walks out into the rain, circling the house to coat my windowsill. Babci leaves the house less and less these days. It used to be that the other women in the village stopped by for a game of bridge or some chin wagging, but now this is rare. The villagers have noticed the trails of fish and lake weeds leading to our house. Nobody around here wants to draw the attention of the dead.

For dinner we have fried green peppers and processed cheese on slabs of buttered toast. I work on my Algebra homework, which Babci calls practicing my arithmetic. My concentration and furrowed brow seem to soothe her. She gets the brandy decanter out, along with a stationary set and an engraved pen. She writes furiously for a while and her sparrow eyes get shiny. I work at my arithmetic until she begins to doze. When she's sleeping, Babci loses her fierceness and looks just like a grandmother. Any grandmother. Like the sort who has rose gardens and bakes cookies and isn't battling dead spirits all the time. I peer over her shoulder and look down at the letter she's writing. *Dear Zofia.* My eyes pick out a few sentences. *I'm so sorry.* I hurry across the words for fear that Babci might wake and catch me snooping. *Please forgive me. Hannah is such a good girl.*

I leave her there at her writing desk, putting an afghan over her shoulders, before going to bed. Whatever she's sorry for, it's probably best left between mother and daughter.

That night I wake to the water witches dancing in the old potato field beside our house. They're doing a *korowody*, a Polish circle dance. Their bodies shimmer and glow in the starlight. Their voices sound like rippling water. Their hair streams about them in weedy banners. They are mostly naked, their skin tinged blue and green and so pale they are lit up like creatures from the deepest parts of the ocean. Some still wear the disintegrating scraps of the clothes they died in. I search for my mother among them. I don't know how long I stand there watching, longing to hear the sweetness of their songs.

"Hannah!" Babci says sharply as I reach to unlock my window. She is there in my doorway in a long nightdress, her thick hair in curlers. "Come away from the window!"

"But look out there," I say. "It's not terrible at all."

"There's nothing there," says Babci. "Come away from the window now, Hannah. And close the drapes. I won't say it again."

Babci sends me to the living room while she double-checks the doors and windows, the toilet seats and the faucets, then she lights the fireplace. She burns prayer candles and plays her old records loud enough to drown out any sounds from outside. I can still hear the singing, the occasional tapping, and some laughter, but I pretend not to notice because my grandmother is so obviously terrified. We sit together in the living room playing Scrabble and pinochle until the sun comes up, when she finally lets me sleep. She pulls the couch away from the wall and close to the uncomfortably warm fireplace. My sleep is sweaty and filled with Rusalki. I am dancing with them. My friends, my sisters, my mother.

•

When I wake up, the house looks different. Uncluttered. Things are missing all over. A statue of the Virgin Mary. Babci's entire collection of beautiful, hand drawn Polish Pysanky eggs. Pictures of me have been taken from the wall. Wreaths of silk flowers. Teacups. Silver spoons. Vases. An embroidered pillow has disappeared from the couch while I was sleeping. And Babci herself is gone.

I run outside, still in my pajamas, and see that Babci has boarded up our windows. The ground around our house is covered in glittering scales that stick to my bare feet. Too many to pick up. Hundreds and hundreds of them, smaller than my pinky nail. There are wheelbarrow tracks in the scales and I follow them down to the lake.

This lake has always been here. From far away I can see the sun shining off its smooth surface. I have grown up less than a half-mile from its haunted waters, but I have only seen it a handful of times. Still, something is terribly out of place.

The wheelbarrow is tipped on its side at the edge of the shore and Babci's treasures are strewn all around the lake like a child's toys. The afghan I had tucked around her is draped across a fallen branch. Silver brushes and ivory combs float on the water, silk flower bouquets and stuffed animals bob along placidly, occasionally tangling in my grandmother's silver hair. She is face down in the water, a red bathrobe on over her nightdress. Her ankles are wrapped in weeds. Tiny silver fish wrinkle the water around her, nibbling at her knuckles and swimming through her hair. Her cherished Pysanky eggs have been smashed into colorful confetti smeared across pages and pages of handwritten letters floating in the water.

I find a tree branch long enough to reach her and struggle against the debris and weeds to pull her to the shore. She's been dead for a while. Her skin is ice cold and chewed away in places. I lay her out on her back and sit with her for a while, looking out at the objects floating on the water.

The sun is high now, and its rays dance on the lake. I am staring out at the debris when a flash of light catches my attention and I see Babci's wedding ring sparkling on a lily pad. Beyond it, an unraveled length of bloody gauze leads down into the depths below. *Zofia*. It's written on the scraps of cloth with permanent marker. *Zofia*. I nudge the body of a porcelain doll over with my foot. The name is scrawled beneath the petticoats. *Zofia*. An open music box floats past and I grab it and examine its underside. *Zofia*. Over and over again. I look closer at the dozens of yellowed letters lapping the shore, tear-stained, stuck to ice, sprinkled with eggshells. They all begin in the same way. *Dear Zofia*. I watch as the ink bleeds into the depths, where the Rusalki, silent now, wait somewhere below.

There is no more laughter, or screeching, or singing. The lake ice has stopped creaking. Everything is silent as fresh snowfall. Twin tears crystallize on my cheeks. Even the Rusalki are quiet now. I imagine them down there, content at last, slurping away at the leftovers of my grandmother's soul.

ONE FOR
THE CROW

In the distance, corn stalks sway against a pale brittle moon. Several large blackbirds have arranged themselves in a row on the fence outside our vegetable garden. Crows. Jackdaws. Grackles. Ravens. Pop says they're the smartest birds around.

"We can't tell them apart from one another, but they can tell us apart," he says. "That gives them the advantage." Pop's engaged in a constant battle with the local avian population. It's a useless struggle, though. Mama won't let him kill any of them on account of bad luck.

"Talulah," Mama says. "Come away from the fields." She stands in the doorway. Her hair is unsheathed and it falls down her white nightgown like buzzard feathers. Her lips are a pale slash of disapproval. Pop says she was beautiful before I was born. "Too many dangerous things out there," she says. "Moons with mouths, devils with pitchforks, lakes that will swallow you whole." She can go on and on.

I don't go to school with other girls my age. I see them through the window sometimes, boys too, swinging their books and talking and laughing. I often sling paper airplanes with messages scrawled on them as the children walk to and from school. Silly messages. Sometimes my name. Sometimes what I've been thinking about behind the closed shutters of my room. Sometimes asking about their lives. I've never gotten any answer.

During the day Mama teaches me things. How to avoid superstitions and evils. Also Latin and French. I recite Shakespearean soliloquies to the corn, bending the stalks backwards as if I were Romeo and Juliet were a swooning, silk-tasseled vegetable. Except our forbidden trysts only take place in the daylight. Once in a while she lets me help outside with the washing or the gardening. This is my favorite thing. To feel the earth buzzing beneath me. As soon as the moon comes out Mama whisks me inside, stokes the hearth, and gives me a task, any task, to keep me busy until Pop comes home and supper is served.

I think we might be rich. Or wealthy at least. Pop's cornfields stretch far across the dusty plains and beneath the heavy-hung skies. During drought or flood they remain fruitful. Mama has lots of jewels and nice dresses but she never wears them. The devil comes calling to see people done up in their finery. That's what she says. There's no place to wear them around here anyway.

"Talulah come in this instant!"

Pop usually brings me presents when he comes back from the market. I have a collection of golden beetles with wings that move and legs that click. They have wheels and gears inside like tiny clocks. My favorite is a giant scarab that buzzes recklessly though the air when I wind it up. I have garlands made of butterflies that dust my room with soft, shimmery sparkles and paper stars that light up my ceiling in a swirling imitation of the world outside.

I have an entire city built out of cardboard that is slowly industrializing my bedroom floor. In the cardboard city, the street lamps turn on at dusk and the people, made of cornhusks, hurry home from work to their corn-dolly families. Origami birds swim above the rooftops and sometimes get swept away in the breeze from my open windows.

Being cooped up in autumn is the hardest, with the crackle of frost and the smell of change. The cawing of the grackles, crows, and jackdaws calls to me. I toss restlessly instead of sleeping. Whenever Mama forgets to lock my shutters I peek at the sepia night outside. The moon slices across the cornfields, growing yolkier as the season turns closer to winter. Each night the branches grow a little barer, until I can practically count the separate leaves on their bony fingers.

"Talulah! Get inside now before you get swallowed up!" Mama calls, and I snap from my reverie in the cornfield.

I look to Pop for a reprieve but he just nods me toward the house with a knowing grin. Pop treats Mama's behavior like it's nothing out of the ordinary. "She's just looking out for you," he calls as I sulk and shuffle my feet. "You know she's got her own way about these things."

Pop is strange in his own way too. He tells stories. "Takes liberties," is what Mama calls it. He likes to say that when I was born they washed me in cold spring water and flowers grew from everything I touched. Flowers that smelled sweeter than any other. And when they combed my baby-fine hair, pearls and rubies tumbled down to the ground like rain.

•

Lately Pop has been looking at my arms. My hands, particularly. Sometimes even my shoulders. The way his gaze traces over them makes me nervous. I wind up my scarab and set it buzzing about the kitchen to distract him. It lands in the pot of oatmeal Mama is cooking and she yells.

"Trinkets and toys! Devilry! Now tell me how much a golden scarab is worth when it's covered in oatmeal?"

Me and Pop keep our mouths shut. He's back to looking at my arms, the hollowed out parts where my shoulders curve into my collarbone. I fold my arms across my chest self-consciously.

"Is it almost time to cut the corn?" I ask.

"Soon," he says, sitting back in his chair and sipping his coffee. He shifts his gaze to the wall. "The Harvest Moon is nearly here."

We still run by tradition around here. Pop never begins the reaping until the moon turns pumpkin-colored and hangs plump and pregnant in the sky. It doesn't matter what the weather is like. It's the secret to his good fortune.

During the harvest, I'm allowed to help during the day. Not just with the shucking but with the swishing of the scythe. The hacking. Releasing the earth from its heavy burden of ripe fruit. Of course the real thrill is being around other people. Pop hires on lots of hands during harvest time. Last year there was a brother and sister, near to me in age, with faces covered in freckles, who wore straw hats and laughed at each other in a way that made my heart ache. After the harvest, I made two corn-dolly replicas of them for my little town.

When Pop leaves for work I help Mama clear the dishes.

"Talulah," she says, "go read the psalms for a little while and then you can help me hang the washing up outside."

She seems to be in a soft mood today, probably because she craves the liquor bottle hidden underneath the sink and wants me out of her hair. I am more than happy to abscond to my bedroom with the promise of autumn sunshine awaiting me.

I have no intention of reading the psalms. Instead I creep over to the windows and pull open the shutters and fill my bedroom with glittering autumn light. My paper village shudders and the butterflies spin through the air in a riot of color. Outside the birds are sitting on our fence again. Today there are even more than usual. Beyond the fence and out in the fields I hear the voices of men. It's past time for all the village children to be at school, but I see a head bobbing up and down over the fence. It's one of the local boys. He walks unhurried, whistling an unfamiliar tune. His hair is glossy and black. His presence disrupts the crows and they scatter and relocate to the top our roof.

His face is square cut and chiseled. He looks a little older than most of the others. There's a familiarity to him, but I can't quite remember where I've seen him. When he turns to look at me I'm rendered immobile. The clash of our eyes shocks me. He smiles and lifts his arm. A paper airplane sails in my window, executes a dizzying sweep of circles, and crashes into an unwitting cornhusk family lounging on a pebble beach. By the time I look back he's gone, and the crows have resettled on the fence.

Inside the folded paper is a name: *Lucian.*

I study the letters. Bold and confident pen strokes. I imagine his hand scrawling them down.

"Talulah," Mama calls.

I hurry and close the shutters. I fold the paper into tiny squares and stick it under my pillow.

"Come on! It's time to do the washing."

He must know my name, too, if he's responding to one of my airplanes. I wonder if he's said it out loud.

Outside the air is chill but the golden sun dusts my skin.

"Gracious," says Mama. "Look at all of these birds. I've never seen so many." She chews the insides of her cheeks.

Pop is wrong. I can tell some of the birds apart. There is a giant grackle bigger than all the rest, and its partner, whose feathers are so black they shine an iridescent green. There is a small jackdaw that's missing an eye, and a crow that hops on one foot. A few of them I can even recognize by their caws.

"We're going to have to do something about them," Mama says. She crosses a hand over her chest. Top to bottom. Left to right.

I pull the tub of water into a patch of sunlight and begin dunking Pop's dusty brown clothes into the sudsy water and rubbing them up and down the washboard. There's a simple delight in the transparent bubbles that rise up around me and burst midair. There's the far off rustle of the corn in the fields. There's the thought of Lucian's name folded up beneath my pillow. I am giddy from the autumn breeze.

"We'll need to put bowls out," says Mama. She's still looking uneasily at the birds. Filling bowls with oil is another one of her superstitions. She says crows are so vain that staring at their own reflection keeps them from getting into devilry. As I wash the clothes and wring them dry for hanging, she goes in and out of the house carrying bowls of oil and setting them on the ground throughout the yard. She puts the most beneath my bedroom window.

That night I peer into the darkness through the slats of my shuttered windows. The moon is fat and swollen. Ready to burst. The heavy corn bends the stalks. The birds are scattered about the yard, gazing at themselves in Mama's bowls. The grass glitters with a light frost.

On my window sill there is a new dolly. One that I didn't

make. It's much rougher than my own corn people. Tied sloppily and missing its arms. I can tell from the bristling skirt and the long plait of tasseled corn-silk hair that it's meant to be a girl. I wonder if it's a gift from Lucian, or a clever trick from the birds.

The yard is filled with hovering black shapes. The giant grackle looks up from the bowl nearest to me and I could swear there's some kind of warning glowing in his eyes.. Lately Mama's been too drunk and distracted to remember to lock the shutters, so I open them just enough to scoop the dolly inside, avoiding the bird's gaze. I close the shutters and put the dolly under my pillow beside the piece of paper. I lie with my head over the name of the black-haired boy, *Lucian*, and fall asleep with the sound of his name on my lips.

•

"I don't know if she should go today," Mama says.

"Elspeth," says Pop. "I'll be twenty yards away from her. Nothing can possibly happen."

I'm all ready. I was up at dawn with the cawing of crows. I have an old pair of work boots on and a dress tattered and stained from previous harvests. In my pocket I have my wind-up scarab, the rough corn dolly, and the paper with Lucian's name on it. Mama has arranged a mason jar full of witch hazel leaves and bright red viburnum berries as a centerpiece on the table. I work some into my braids as they argue.

"I don't care how many birds you saw yesterday," Pop says. "They're just birds. They come to eat the corn. Name me one farmer who doesn't have to deal with them."

"They've been watching the house," Mama says.

Pop gets up from the table abruptly. "Enough of the doom and gloom already." He tosses me some gloves and smiles a kingly smile. "Wear these. I don't want you to hurt your hands. Are you ready for the harvest, Talulah?"

I nod. This is something me and Pop share. Probably that's what makes Mama so worried.

"She's a farmer's daughter," says Pop, as if that settles it. We say goodbye to Mama, taking our lunches and our canteens, and head out towards the cornfields.

The workers are waiting for Pop, standing in a line watching silently. They remind me of the birds. Some of them really look like crows, all hunched over and hungry. They watch me and Pop approach with careful eyes, waiting for his instruction.

"Harvest time!" Pop shouts, and there are some vague hurrahs. The men are glad to have work, but their faces show a slight resentment at laboring in someone else's fields. Still, the sway of tradition and the promise of a plentiful crop wins out. There is a zing to the air that makes my skin ripple.

Hooky! Hooky! The shouts resound around the assembled throng. I want to yell too but I know Pop wouldn't like that.

I don't see the freckled twins but my eyes pick out Lucian right away. He's leaning on a chaff-cutter beside the wagon and staring straight at me with a little smile. My insides flutter. His eyes look wicked. He tips his head in my direction and I glance quickly at Pop, but he doesn't notice.

"What are we waiting for?" Pop asks. "If you don't have tools of your own, grab one out of the wagon. The women will bring down cider and refreshments in a few hours."

Inside the wagon is an assortment of sickles, fagging-hooks, chaff-cutters, hoes, and winnowing baskets. I take a sickle and a corn husker. The blade gleams in the morning light.

The workers scatter into the tall rows of corn. I look for Lucian but he has disappeared.

"Talulah," Pop calls. "Remember to stay close."

I wave my sickle at him and smile. All around me the swish and crackle of the reaping has begun.

Inside the cornfields I become a much smaller version of myself. Stalks reach up over my head, closing off the sky. Down the narrow aisles the shadows of men swing sickles. Women scurry after them, picking up the golden ears and silken tassels and stacking them in their baskets.

I make a game of it, losing myself in the tallest parts of the cornfield. *Swish. Swish. Blade through stalk. Thump. Thump. Corn to earth.* It's almost trancelike. Then I hear whistling ahead of me and around me. Lucian appears from behind a cluster of cornstalks.

"Talulah," he says. His eyes are not dark at all. They are the gold of the cornfields.

"I'm not supposed to talk to anyone," I tell him. My gaze wanders off to the waving tops of the corn. The shuddering leaves. The silver curve of my sickle.

"Is this your first harvest?" he asks.

I swoop my sickle through the air, neatly taking down several stalks just below the ears. They fall to the ground in a series of crackles and thumps.

"Of course it isn't. These are your father's fields." He smiles when he says this.

I want to ask him if he put the dolly on my windowsill. And why he answered my paper airplane letter. And how many of them he's read. Instead I stand there shivering. The air between us glitters with the crystals of frozen morning mist. A woman comes by with a winnowing basket to pick up the wake of cut corn behind me. She's singing to herself in an off-key voice.

One for the cut worm
One for the crow
One for the blackbird
And three to grow

The words are from an old rhyme. Every farmer's daughter knows it. But it's about the planting, not the reaping. The basket woman nods at me and continues on, her voice echoing down the rows of corn. I look to Lucian but he has disappeared among the tall stalks as if he were never there.

I begin cutting again. The swoosh of blade through stalk soothes me. The relief of the cold earth under my feet as each ear tumbles to the ground. My arms ache, but it's a good ache. Mama shows up with a few of the other village women halfway through the day. She has a gown on, dark red and regal. The harvest is the only event she dresses for all year. Her hair is done up into coiled braids. I'm always surprised to see her like this. It gives me a glimpse of the young woman she must have been.

The women have brought carts of refreshments. Hot cider, slabs of meat, loaves of bread, and steaming potatoes. The workers line up, dust-streaked faces, blackened feet, and blistered hands. Mama oversees the feasting like a queen even though she didn't prepare any of it. She's been into the whisky, I can tell. Her eyes are shining and her cheeks are flushed. It takes her a little while to spot me in the crowd.

"Don't stand in line like you're common," she says, taking my arm and pulling me aside. She hands me a big plate of food and rakes her eyes over me. "Have you had enough for the day then? Are you ready to come home?"

"Mama, please. I'm fine."

She checks my hands beneath my gloves and examines my arms for cuts or gashes. I can feel the eyes of the others on me.

"Elspeth, leave her be," Pop says loudly. "This is a part of who she is. You know that as well as I do."

Mama's lips flatten into slashes. She rejoins the other women in overseeing the food and drink. I wander a little way off into the corn and sit down to eat away from her broody gaze. The rest of the workers keep a careful distance.

Lucian appears as suddenly as he had vanished and sits down beside me. The corn stalks around us are whispering in papery voices.

"I wouldn't," I tell him. "If either one of my parents walks over here, you're as good as done for."

"Your parents don't frighten me," he says. He pushes a mug of cider into my hands.

"Why do you suppose they keep you locked up all the time?"

Nobody has ever asked me that question, though I haven't had many conversations with people from the outside world. It helps to pretend we're two of my corn dollies. The words come easier. "Mama thinks the world is dangerous and full of the Devil. Pop's just protective."

The cider burns down my throat and my skin begins to tingle. The sun seems to shine a little brighter. Lucian's eyes are positively glowing.

"Do you think the world is full of the Devil?" he asks.

"I have no idea what the world is full of. I've barely seen it."

"So see it," he says.

The sun rests on my skin and I let his smile melt the thought of my parents away. We grin at each other in the dust for a moment, then Lucian gets up and offers me his hand.

•

We spend the rest of the afternoon running through tunnels of corn, having cutting contests, drinking cider, and playing silly games. When the sky dims and the cries of hooky, hooky start up again, I hear Pop yelling my name but I don't care. I feel dizzy and alive. As the glorious orange moon rises in the sky, the basket women collect the last of the corn from the ground. Lucian pulls me through the narrow tunnels of empty stalks to the edge of the field, where we watch in the shadows as the harvesters light a massive bonfire and assemble the corn into piles. I've never seen this part of the harvest before. I've never been allowed to stay out this long. I see Pop among the men, scanning the crowd for me. He looks wobbly on his feet.

"This is a husking bee," says Lucian. I feel closer to him than anyone else in the world.

"What's that?" I ask.

"It's a race to find the red corn."

As night sets in and shadows fall across the cornfield, Lucian looks different. In the sun he was a carefree farm boy, but now his features are mysterious. His eyes flash red in the bonfire light. Men are gathered around giant piles of corn with their shucking tools at the ready.

"Whoever finds the red ear of corn," Lucian says, "gets to kiss the girl of his choice. That's how most courtships start."

A few people have begun playing fiddles and some dance around the fire. Pop is a staggering silhouette calling out my name. I look up at the lights of our house on the hill and see Mama walking down with a lantern, no doubt to bring me home. The men are getting ready to start the husking. When I look back to Lucian, he's staring up and down my arms.

"Don't you want to be in the husking bee?" I ask.

Lucian shakes his head. The firelight dances across his face. He reaches up casually and pulls down a stalk someone missed. He takes a small knife from his back pocket and slices off the ear of corn. I hear Pop getting closer, stumbling through the corn. Lucian peels the tassels down slowly and, instead of the usual rich yellow, the kernels are a deep red. Like beating hearts. When Lucian looks up and smiles at me, I have the sudden feeling that this has all been fated since the moment I glimpsed him from my window. There's too much knowledge in that smile. The corn and knife drop from his hands and he leans even closer to claim his kiss, but when he grabs my arms to pull me in, the feel of his skin on my skin galvanizes me into action.

I take off running through the cornfields as fast as I can. Lucian chases me. We weave in and out of the tunnels of severed stalks. The Harvest Moon crawls along the horizon.

I run into Lucian and we tumble to the ground. We kiss with mouths full of dirt, our bodies smashed together. He smells like cider and sweet corn. We roll around and at some point the golden scarab in my pocket gets jostled and kicks into action, its little legs clicking, its wings buzzing as it swoops off drunkenly into the night. I have forgotten about everything but flesh and earth. We lie on our backs and stare up at the glowing sky when a shadow falls over the moon.

Pop is standing over us. His expression is terrifying. I scramble to my feet, but Lucian takes his time. When he's standing fully, he smiles at Pop. They are close to the same height.

All of a sudden the moon seems in a hurry. It rises above the corn and watches with a marmalade gaze. Clouds race across the stars. The world seems to swirl. Everything is too familiar. This place. This night. This moment. I don't know which direction to panic in.

"It's just a little fun," says Lucian.

"How could you?" Pop says to me. "I've given you everything."

Given me what, I wonder. Corn people aren't the same as real ones.

Pop steps closer to me and Lucian. I can smell the whiskey in his tears. His curved blade reflects hot orange as he lifts it toward the moon.

•

The earth around me is still wet with blood, but my arms have been tightly bound with cornhusks, just above the elbows, to stanch the flow. The pain it takes to struggle to my feet is nearly unbearable. I'm dizzy from blood loss but, instinctually, I walk, following an assortment of birds flying just ahead. Grackles. Ravens. Jackdaws. Crows. Sometimes they swoop down to check on me as I stumble after them. I wonder how I will catch myself if I fall.

Cornfields give way to grassy hills. The birds find puddles for me to drink from, until finally we come to a stream. The air is slightly warmer. I have walked for so long that my boots are worn down through the soles and, while most of my body has shrunk, my belly has grown large and swollen. Beside the stream there is a copse of trees. I am so exhausted and grateful to find anything like shelter that I drink from the stream until I feel full, and fall asleep in the soft moss beside the water.

I wake after what feels like days, a cold beak against my ear. The grackle and his mate are watching. There is a pile of berries beside me, and some small fish. I struggle to sit up, but the female grackle with the iridescent feathers hops over to me instead. She nudges my mouth open and drops a beak-full of sweet berries in. Then the fish.

The birds build me a giant nest of twigs and moss, insulated enough to keep out the cold. It is a tremendous feat of skill and craftsmanship. The jackdaws, the more mischievous of the bunch, go on a pillaging raid—I don't know where—and return with warm blankets and clothes to replace the tattered shreds I removed when we first reached the stream. The ravens bring me rabbits and mice, which I usually decline. The iridescent grackle changes the wrappings on my arms each day, until my wounds are no longer bloody and raw. The crows fill the days and nights with their chatter. I think they are singing lullabies. But the grackles are the keenest. They salvage broken baby dolls, stolen rattles, and scraps of soft, pink fabric and leave them beside me, as if they know it's a girl that is coming.

We settle into a routine together. We bathe in the same stream. Eat the same food. I talk to them, to let them know how much I need them, and so I don't forget the sound of my own voice. At night I curl up in my nest, my knees tucked high, cradling my belly, while the birds roost in the trees around me.

When the baby finally comes, the pain slices through the blankness inside me. She's small and pink and wrinkled. The beaks and claws of my avian midwives seem suddenly sharp against her soft skin. Her body spasms with furious, shuddering gasps, and then screams that seem to split the sky in two. I want to soothe her, but I don't know anything about babies. The grackles help tie off the cord with their beaks, and then I lift her to my chest with my stubs, even though she's still wet and slippery.

The grackles start a fire and I crawl on my knees to the stream to clean up before other animals smell us. The water is clear and cold and I wriggle down into the water first for fear of dropping her. Then, carefully, I dip her in. She squeals. As soon as her tiny toes touch the water, flowers of every kind and color bubble up to the surface. Water lilies, roses, hyacinths, and laurel go floating down the little stream, perfuming the cool air. I have no hands to scrub her with, so I use the soft moss that grows along the bank to sponge her. Flowers bloom all around us. For a moment, I'm lost in the sheer wonder of it all. And this is when she slides out of my grasp. She slips under the water, trailing daisies as she sinks down noiselessly.

I stare down at my daughter as if through a glass case. I try to wrestle her back up, thrashing my stumps around as the stream fills with flowers. I duck my head under and try to get ahold of her flesh with my teeth, but they don't find any purchase on her smooth skin. Pain shoots down my arms. Real pain. Unbearable. I try to paddle deeper only to bob up again helplessly as she sinks farther into the water.

The phantom limbs of my amputated arms throb as she slips away from me. The memory of the scythe biting through my flesh. The gleam of a moonlit smile. Pop standing over me angry and tall. And that's when I realize there is flesh beneath my pain. Real flesh. Solid and tender. I curl my fingers around a tiny torso and pull us both out of the water. She's alive. Coughing and sputtering, but alive. I set her down and pat her back gently to help get the water up—pat her back with fully formed limbs as new and pink as my daughter's. Flowers stick to my arms and hands, and new blooms form in the soft grass around us. I pick my daughter up and cradle her in my arms by the warmth of the fire.

The birds solemnly march past us in a mock processional. My daughter gasps and fusses and gurgles up at them. Water dribbles from the creases of her mouth, but she doesn't cry. Not even when the giant grackle and his mate drop two gifts in the grass beside us. The first is a necklace made of blood-red corn kernels threaded onto a single string. The second is the armless corn dolly. The grackle fixes those glowing eyes on mine again and I'm transported back to a night that seems like lifetimes ago, when I was just a girl, wondering about the world, looking out from my open window.

Then their wings begin to open and close in unison like folded paper airplanes. The air fills with the whir of gentle flapping. One by one the birds lift into the sky, crying out as they circle above us. My daughter finds her voice at the same time, releasing a high pitched wailing. She shrieks with life as the entire congregation makes their last swirls and begin winging away from us, blowing my hair back from my face in wet tangles. I look down at my daughter and our eyes meet for the first time. Hers are the blue-blind eyes of a newborn. The sky is empty, save for the fall of black, downy feathers.

THE CHURCH OF THE LIVING GOD & RESCUE HOME FOR DIVINE ORPHANS

How I came to be born with a sun inside of me is a mystery. Of course the sisters say it was Jesus-ordained, but I'm not totally convinced. I gave my mother terrible pain and heartburn during her pregnancy. I emerged burning hot from the womb, covered not in the traditional afterbirth, but a glowing, golden capsule that burst immediately and scalded everyone in the room. My mother survived the ordeal with a couple second-degree burns. Once I'd been examined, it was determined that I had, indeed, been born with a sun inside of me. It caused a tremendous rift between my parents. My father accused my mother of all sorts of abominations and infidelities, so in the end, she sacrificed me to save their marriage and I was sent here. I know all of this because the nuns told me.

I live in a special sanctuary for girls like me or, rather, girls who are un-like everyone else. We're the ordained charges of The Church of the Living God and Rescue Home for Divine Orphans. Despite the name, not all of us are orphans. The nuns have saved plenty of girls from parents who exploited their gifts or were afraid of their perceived curses. This place is full of sad stories.

My best friend, Milagros, has long, dark hair, delicate features, and skin the color of desert sand. She squeezes semi-precious crystals out of her eyes twice a day. Beryl, amethyst, emerald, the especially painful rough-ruby, and even the occasional diamond. Her mother used to sit her on a stool in the town square and charge admission while Milagros squeezed out crystals on demand. Now she is nearly blind and her pupils are scarred white in places. Jagged lines etch out from her eyes. She's still pretty in a tortured kind of way. Most of us are.

We share a room together because my glowing in the dark doesn't bother her. On one wall we have arranged her crystals into rainbow-hued assortments on some of the kitchen's old wooden spice racks. The citrine is my favorite. It gleams bright gold when I handle it. Milagros doesn't care if I touch the crystals, though they are worth a small fortune. She has given many of them to the nuns, who arrange them on altars and call them gifts from the Lord. In the mornings, Milagros and I wake up early to the ringing of church bells. She loves the feel of the morning breeze at the window and stands with her face turned into it, sometimes squeezing out a gem or two. I worry that our room is too stifling with all the heat I give off while I sleep, but Milagros never complains. She is from somewhere warm and far south of here. A place with ripe, green rain and drunken butterflies.

"Girls, girls!" says Sister Annika, swooshing into our rooms and clapping her hands in a giant rush of excitement. "We have a visitor today! A prince is coming!"

Despite the excitement, we all set about our morning chores. Milagros and I are on breakfast duty with Marta. She's our resident mesmerist. The secret is in her hair, which she keeps tightly bound up in a white cloth when the sisters aren't showcasing her talent. Men and women alike fall into trancelike states at the sight of her cascading golden tresses. When Marta first arrived at the convent she had shaved her own head. She doesn't much care for attention of any kind. Her features are lovely, but always grim with memories of something she refuses to reveal. When I look at Marta I know that burning hot skin is not such a terrible thing after all. It's only a physical condition. Marta has a sickness of the soul.

I ask if she's excited about the Prince's visit.

"No," says Marta, swirling the pot of gruel. "I won't be attending. I don't care for princes. They are a self-righteous and condescending bunch."

"I don't stand a chance," says Milagros. "My eyes are a horror. No matter how much wealth I produce, I get uglier and uglier."

Marta gives her a comfortless hug. "The sooner you stop caring, the better off you'll be."

I remain silent through this exchange. I am not the most beautiful or dainty girl at the home. When I drink water it sizzles in my belly and smoke comes out of my nose and ears. I am embarrassed for wanting a prince. The girl who swallowed the sun. I have never felt holy.

•

Milagros and I pretend we are not in direct competition. I put flowers in her hair, and she tries to do the same for me, but they wilt immediately. I apply makeup to help conceal the scars around her eyes. She dusts a fine, glimmery powder over my face and it melts into puddles. My dress is paper thin to keep me from overheating, and I carry a golden fan with peacock feathers on it to try to regulate my temperature. When I am excited I burn much hotter than usual.

"Girls, come down," Sister Annika calls. "It is a proper holy ball we are having. The Prince wants to see all of you. And there are other guests, besides."

Milagros and I giggle, holding each other's trains. Our slippers make delicate clickety-clicks that echo off the stone walls as we descend the stairs. Although she is practically a sister to me, I feel a momentary flash of envy. She looks extraordinarily delicate and beautiful in my warm glow.

Already assembled are Flora, Juniper, Melusine, and Gabriella. All of the girls are excited and awkward, except for Gabriella, who lives in perpetual slumber inside a glass case. She washed ashore somewhere a few years ago and was immediately sent to the nuns. The nuns de-barnacled the glass case and set right to work giving her beauty treatments. Her pale face is perfectly composed and her silk dress is adorned with wildflowers.

We are all dressed in our finest in order to capture the attention of the Prince. There is crinoline, lace, and tulle everywhere. Candles and incense burn, and harpists play soothing and sacred songs. Dukes and duchesses watch us from the recesses of the extravagant room. Decked in layers of blue velvet, the Prince stands in the center, handsome and arrogant, as if he's used to others positioning themselves around him.

"Here they are," says Sister Annika as Milagros and I enter. She introduces us by our holy titles. The Girl Who Swallowed the Sun and The Girl Who Rains Diamonds From Her Eyes. The Girl Who Sleeps Like the Dead. The Girl Who Comes From the Sea.

The Prince's eyes glide over Milagros and I. He smiles and takes both our hands in turn. When he raises mine for a kiss, blisters form on his lips. But he is a prince, so he doesn't drop it quickly or act surprised. Instead, he stares as if trying to pinpoint where exactly the light is coming from. It's everywhere. "I have sunshine flowing through my veins," I say.

Sister Annika sweeps over and corrals us with the rest of the girls.

"Now," she says, "Juniper plays a beautiful minuet. And Flora dances like a winged angel." She looks at Milagros and then at me, trying to determine how to explain our finest traits. She asks Juniper to play a sad song in hopes the girls will be moved to tears. In addition to being a pianist, Juniper cries blood. And it doesn't take much for Milagros to squeeze out gems when she feels appropriately moved.

I take a seat at the window while the dukes and duchesses peer at me. A few ladies are waving paper fans at their faces. It's true that I heat up a room. The sisters are always complaining that I cause undue wear and tear, charring the fine wood floors and furniture, but I must haul in a good bit of coin, because they keep me around. Even now, the sisters pull the heavy drapes closed and trust me to fill the room with a soft golden glow.

Juniper strikes up a melody and the assorted guests look on. The Prince watches us all. Milagros casts her eyes toward her feet to conceal her scars beneath heavy sweeps of lashes. Melusine hides her webbed hands behind her back. I know how much she longs to get out of here. The ocean calls to her every night.

Although we have been saved, the doors to our rooms are locked tightly at night. The sisters say the world isn't safe for divine orphans. Given how most of us ended up here, perhaps they're right. Princes are an obvious escape route, and lucrative one for the nuns.

The Prince is staring at me. Juniper's piano playing has not produced any blood or jewels, but he doesn't seem to mind. He crosses the room. "Would you care to dance?" he asks.

Milagros quivers beside me, but he's looking into my eyes. His are a frosty blue.

I look to the sisters for approval. Sister Annika nods her head.

We begin to waltz. The air between us eddies in hot and cold swells. His hands are gloved, so I don't worry about burning them. We dance for a while and he examines my arms, my skin. He removes a glove and lays a gentle hand to my cheek. His touch leaves a feather-light frost across my skin.

"What's your real name?" asks the Prince.

"Eliana," I say. I feel as if I have given up a secret. My cheeks don't flush, they burn.

Some of the dukes and duchesses have joined us on the dance floor. A few of the girls are invited to dance. Milagros is still alone, standing by the glass box containing Gabriella. I want to go to her, but it would be rude to stop dancing with a prince. I thought by now he'd be uncomfortably warm, but he seems to be enjoying himself.

"Do you want to know my name?" he asks. His blistered lips curve into a small smile.

"Yes," I say.

We do some swirly move that I vaguely remember learning from one of the Sisters. The air behind us curls into ribbons.

"I'm North," he says, and I love that name as he says it. I imagine falling snowflakes, dripping icicles, and frozen seas.

"North." I turn the word over on my tongue and it sizzles.

Our bodies are nearly touching now. I am fevered and fluttery.

Then Sister Annika swoops in. "Your Highness, I must insist that she rest," she says. "She is frail and she overheats easily."

The Prince lets me go, and I am surrounded by a circle of nuns who fan me and pat my skin with cold compresses. I can't see the dance floor around their plump and bustling bodies. This is a strategic maneuver, I'm sure of it. It's only later, after testimonials have been given, people have been saved, and miracles have been witnessed—long after the Prince and his guests have said goodbye, filling the sisters' coffers with tokens of their appreciation—that I am allowed to join the other girls again.

We adjourn to the room that Gabriella and Juniper share. Since Gabriella sleeps in her glass case, there is an extra bed for us to gather on. The room is warm with all of us crammed in together.

Flora unbraids Melusine's hair while I change Gabriella from her ball finery into a soft dressing gown. It's like undressing a doll. I lay a blanket over her and close the lid of the glass case almost all the way, leaving a crack so she can listen. She must get awfully bored in there.

"We each got to dance with him," Juniper says. She opens the window for some breeze and her bird flies in. It follows her around everywhere, its plumage bright in the moonlight. "Nobody as long as you, Eliana, but he danced with Milagros second longest." The bird flutters over to her shoulder, head cocked inquisitively. When visitors come, the sisters chase her bird off with brooms, but it always returns once they're gone

Juniper is the youngest of the orphans. Freckles dust her pale skin and her face is girlish and sweet—all the more surprising when her eyes fill with blood. The sisters found her grief-stricken in the forest, covered in her own crimson tears, the bird perched on her shoulder. The sisters say there is a secret inside her that hasn't unraveled yet. Until then, her bloody tears are yet more proof that the Holy Spirit resides inside of us.

"What did he say to you, Eliana?" Melusine asks. She sniffs at the breeze for the smell of salted waters. Her green-tinted webbed fingers stretch reflexively. "He was quiet when he danced with me."

I shrug. I don't want to give them his name. It sits close to my heart like a secret. "Nothing really. Only pleasantries."

"Milagros?"

Milagros gazes dreamily out the window. "Same. Pleasantries, I suppose. And some questions about our... conditions."

"Our divinity," Juniper corrects. She is still young enough to believe whatever the sisters say.

"Our divinity," agrees Milagros. "And he asked me how the nuns treated us. How we lived. If we had enough to eat or knew how to read."

My jealousy flares up so quickly I can't control it. A burst of heat escapes me. The other girls turn to look at me.

Flora inspects her wings to make sure they aren't singed. "What's that about?" she huffs, moving away from me on the bed. "You know how quickly I catch fire!"

"Sorry," I say. "I must be coming down with something." But really I am envious of Milagros, her spill of dark hair and the gentle smile on her face. "Did he tell you his name?" I ask.

Milagros blinks. "No."

I feel vindicated, triumphant, but only for a moment. Milagros is my best friend. Practically my sister. We've shared a room since we were little girls. We've shared every part of our lives. Only Milagros knows about my parents, my lack of faith, my dreams and desires. My triumph quickly turns to shame.

Melusine lets out a deep-sea sigh. "I'll never get out of here," she says. "I'll be a dry-skinned, web-fingered old maid before I know it. Let's make a pact: whoever escapes first will come back for the others."

"*Melusine*," Juniper scolds.

But most of us have thoughts that parallel Melusine's. You can only fool yourself into believing you are a divine miracle for so long.

"There's a difference between being saved and being free," Flora explains to Juniper. The nuns clip her wings regularly. They say it's for grooming purposes. They say flying is dangerous. That she was given her gift to turn blasphemers into believers, not for selfishly navigating the perils of the open sky.

In their daily sermons, the nuns preach about a world that would use us to cruel advantage. They say the safest place for us is within the confines of the home. Perhaps they're only delivering God's truth, but that doesn't stop us from imagining something more.

We form a circle and join hands, all except for Juniper, who refuses, and Gabriella, who can't, and agree that we are in this together, that if one of us gets out, we vow to free the rest. Then the church bells begin ringing, signaling lights out for all of us. I close the lid of Gabriella's glass box and say goodnight to the girls. Milagros and I walk back to our room together. Despite the vow of unity with the other girls, between the two of us it feels as though something has shifted.

"I have a secret," she says. "I'm in love with the Prince."

Her declaration makes me hot and angry.

When she gets no response from me she turns toward the window. "He kissed me Eliana. After you left. I think he has serious intentions."

While she stands at our window staring out at a sliver of moon, I toss and turn, hot in my bed. I eye the collection of jewels that line our walls with narrowed eyes. I'm unusually annoyed by the rainbow prisms. Milagros is wrong. The Prince isn't interested in her. It's me that he wants. I'm sure of it.

I have hardly slept by the time morning comes. Bells. It's constant bells here. Enough to drive anyone crazy. My skin is warmer than usual. Outside the sky is the color of robin's eggshells cracked apart by the sun. Milagros is still at the window, smiling.

We go downstairs together to help Marta in the kitchen.

"How was the ball?" she inquires politely.

"Wonderful," says Milagros. She doesn't look so tortured this morning. The radiant curve of her lips fuels the ferocious burn in my belly.

Marta narrows her eyes at her. "I know that look."

Milagros holds out her hand in answer. In her palm is a single gemstone. It is an opaque shimmery blue that conjures images of flowering vines of morning glory, summer stars, and birdsong. It is smooth and polished already.

"That's different," I say, wondering why she didn't show it to me when we were alone.

Marta examines it.

"I found it on my pillow this morning," says Milagros. "I didn't even feel it."

"Happiness," says Marta. "There are a million different ways to cry."

I try to keep my composure by checking the bread in the oven. A true friend would be delighted, I tell myself. Milagros goes out to serve the nuns their breakfast, leaving me alone with Marta.

"Does that gem look like love?" I ask.

"No," she says abruptly. She stops cutting onions and looks at me as closely as she did the stone. "Why do you ask?"

I shrug. "I was just wondering. What is it like then?"

"What do you think it's like?"

"I don't know." I try to sound casual. "Maybe like ripples of hot and cold. Breathlessness. Heart palpitations."

"That's pure animal instinct," says Marta. "It's called fight or flight. That's what happens when animals face predators. If you ever feel like that, your body is telling you to run."

Marta knows a lot but she doesn't know everything. I've read plenty of books. I've listened to enough stories. She goes back to chopping onions and her eyes don't even water. Marta's made of stone. What does she really know about love?

Later, during our studies, we are all distracted. Sister Annika can tell. "Let's take a constitutional," she says, and leads us outside into the gated gardens of the chapel grounds. Each girl has her own statue here, except for Juniper. She'll get hers soon. The nuns are waiting for her to blossom into adolescent glory.

Melusine is immortalized in a spray of marble ocean foam and shining scales leading down from her navel. Marta is poised with her hair flowing out around her in ripples and waves. My own statue is haloed by slatted golden sunbeams, and I'm shown gripping my stomach as if I have indigestion. It's not my most flattering likeness, but on overcast days the nuns place candles inside a hollow compartment in my head and my eyes become twin beams of light. My mouth a gaping, golden grin. Milagros' statue is lovely and woeful and encrusted with rivers of jeweled tears.

The nuns charge visitors entry into the gardens most days. It's only on rare occasions like this that we are allowed to come outside. Together we walk among the birds and flowers that accompany our statues. Mine is adorned with brilliant yellow riots of star-shaped Clematis Helios—the flower of the sun. Milagros' statue is surrounded by flowers that attract butterflies and hummingbirds. For a while, we make a game out of catching the butterflies and setting them free. I urge mine up over the tall hedges and out into the world. Juniper's bird has followed us and does somersaults of ecstasy in the sunshine.

After a while we disperse. I lounge in a pile of soft grass, breathing in the smell of the world beyond the gardens. I doze a little and dream of castles hung with icicles. Frost on my lips. Gemstones that pierce hearts. When I wake up Sister Annika is shaking me.

"Eliana," she says. "You have a visitor."

It's the Prince. I know this so surely that I am not surprised when I see a white horse with velvet draping waiting outside the chapel. The fluttering starts as soon as I see him. The bouts of hot and cold. He stands beside the horse, greedily drinking up the sight of my glowing skin.

"North," I say.

"Eliana." He smiles and bows. Cool air ripples past me and I shiver. His face is smooth as glass. His features are composed and perfect. It's his eyes that excite me. "I've asked the sisters for your hand in marriage," he says.

I don't care what Marta says. This is love. I don't care what

Milagros' dream-tears look like. This is love. Love makes water freeze and planets crash. Love feels like frost covering the sun. I never cry, not even tears of joy—my body evaporates moisture too quickly—but if I could, I'm sure I would be weeping jewels of happiness that rival any Milagros has ever produced.

Suddenly Juniper's bird dive-bombs my head, snatching up bits of hair, and ruining the moment. The sisters try to chase it away. "Come on," says Sister Annika. "Let's get you ready."

I've said yes without even realizing it.

•

My room is empty except for the nuns. Milagros has moved into Juniper's room temporarily, they say. I ask why I'm being kept apart from the other girls.

"You'll see them at the wedding," says Sister Annika.

Until then I am kept on twenty-four-hour watch. No princes. No divine orphans. The sisters play rummy on a card table they've set up in the middle of the room. They chant prayers around the clock. Juniper's little bird pecks at the closed window.

My wedding will be a spectacle: royal, divine, and bizarre. The sisters have insisted it be held in our chapel and, for a fee, it is open to anyone. The event will keep them prosperous for years to come. In the morning, the gardens will fill with visitors from far and wide. I'll look down from my window to see my statue bedecked in flowered wreaths and streamers. I will be similarly festooned, with swathes of silk, lace, and ribbon.

"I want to see Milagros," I say, but the nuns shake their heads over their cards. They are betting on gold coins and precious gems from the coffer.

"Get some rest," they say, then continue betting.

My sleep is fitful. I stare at the ceiling, thinking about Milagros. I toss and turn to the sound of shuffling cards, clinking coins, and the bird's persistent tapping.

·

Juniper is my flower girl. I can tell by the way she distributes flower petals, her elfin features set deep in concentration, that she is taking her job very seriously. The other orphans stand off to the side, divine bridesmaids. Their gowns absorb the light that fills the chapel, streaming through the stained glass ceilings. They make an amazing spectacle. Marta's hair is unbound in rich golden coils, stealing the gazes of most of the men in the room, although her expression remains cold and indifferent. Melusine's dress looks like it's made of sea foam, setting off the green shimmer in her complexion. But it's Milagros that I'm desperate to see. Her gown is a stiff, corseted brocade encrusted with jewels. Her eyes are cast downward and her skin is unusually pale. As I watch, she sways on her feet until Flora steadies her, wings flapping slightly. I tell myself it's only because the nuns laced her dress too tightly.

The melodies of harpsichords carry me between crowds of eager onlookers. The rooms and gardens are packed to bursting. I step slowly, hot and dizzy beneath thousands of curious stares, inhaling a heady combination of incense and flowers. Everything swirls around me. I keep focused on North, standing calmly at the altar beside Sister Annika, who will perform the ceremony. He holds the promise of freedom. The thrill of the cold. I move my legs forward despite the fluttery excitement he produces in me.

I'm halfway up the aisle when things begin to go awry. First, Juniper's bird crashes through the stained glass and begins dive-bombing Sister Annika. One of the nuns intervenes, hits it with a wooden plank, and the bird flutters to the ground. The nun carries it off, unconscious, and this is what starts Juniper crying—not a sprinkling of bloody tears, but torrents that gush down her face as if the floodgates of hell have just lifted. She drops her basket of petals and runs to join the other girls. The crowd swells with excitement. Blood splashes all over Flora's angel wings and flows in rivulets through the cracks in the stone floor of the chapel. Flora releases Milagros and tries to push Juniper away, which only makes her cry harder. The sisters proclaim this a divine blessing of the Lord and carry on with the service. I want to join my sisters. Comfort Juniper. Check on Milagros, who appears woozy and unsteady. But I am now at the altar. North takes my chin between his fingers and directs my gaze to his eyes. I'm trapped and delirious. *Love*, I think. *This is love.*

We exchange our vows before the streams of blood, the horrified and fascinated crowd, and the fat, smiling nuns. Sister Annika pronounces us man and wife. "You may now kiss the bride," she says and, just as our lips meet, there is a deafening crash. Milagros has fainted into Gabriella's glass box. They both lie in the shattered glass. Now Milagros, shocked into consciousness, begins to cry as well. A particularly large gem forces its way out of her eye, contorting her face and popping out to land on her cheek like a black tourmaline beetle. The jewels continue to force their way out, one after another, spilling across her cheeks in a steady flow of despair and pain. I try to run to her side, but North holds tight to my wrist. The floor is covered with jewels and blood and glass.

"This isn't your life anymore," he says. He touches my cheek and I get chilblains. An itch is creeping up my fingers where

North is holding them. When I look down at my hands they are snow white and threaded with blue veins. The ring on my finger resembles an iceberg.

Marta tries to console Milagros and help ease the jewels from her eyes. Milagros is bleeding now, too. I am sure she will never see again. The sisters whip the crowd into a holy frenzy, shouting prayers and directing the fiasco to seem like a divine blessing. There are people falling down everywhere. People anointing themselves with Juniper's tears. People scrabbling for gemstones. It is less a wedding than a nightmare.

"Let's go," says North. "You are a princess now."

He leads me through the riotous crowd, into a carriage, and pulls the drapes closed around us. Nobody comes to say goodbye as we leave. Not the nuns. Not the orphans. We sit in each other's silence.

I realize that he smells like the air before a snowfall. I realize he's my husband. I do my best not to think about the scene I left behind me. The friends I've left behind. I will find a way to honor our pact. I will return to set them free.

When the silence becomes too much, North touches my neck with his ungloved fingers and I begin to tremble, lost in the sensation of flesh, the contrast of hot and cold, the realization that burning is the same at either extreme. By the time we're finished, his lips are blistered, his chest marred with burns. There is frostbite between my legs.

"A witch told me I was cursed," he says, in the painful afterglow of our shared closeness. "She said I was frozen solid. That I would never find any woman who could make me feel."

"Feel what?" I ask.

"Anything," he says. "But she was wrong. I can feel you."

He arranges the inside of the carriage so we're able to sit

together comfortably, using a fur coat to shield his skin from the heat.

"Why did you pretend to take such an interest in Milagros?" I ask. "That mess inside the chapel would not have happened if you hadn't. My sisters were hurt."

He seems surprised. "The nuns asked me to. It was a part of our agreement."

I don't know why I'm shocked. More tears means more gifts from the Lord. At the Church of the Living God and Rescue Home for Divine Orphans, heartbreak is the ultimate tithing. It's what keeps the place running.

"I knew we would be married as soon as I kissed your hand," he whispers. "You give me blisters. Your friend doesn't."

North's chill seeps through me, a kind of relief that soon turns to numbness. I rest my head on the furs covering his shoulder. *I'm not alone*, I remind myself. *I'm a princess now.*

•

Some things seem much clearer looking backward. For example, the moment in the kitchen when Marta tried to explain love. I know it now. It's pain. It's excruciating and mad and destructive. It hurts to be around my husband and it hurts to be without him. Every day I feel little pieces of my own soul slipping away.

We live in a frozen lighthouse atop a frozen sea. Somewhere so far north I don't think it's on a map. The wind here cuts straight through me and the sun hardly ever emerges from behind the thick gray clouds. Early in our marriage, North built a tall ice wall to keep the howling wind from knocking me off the bridge that connects the top of the lighthouse to our sleeping chambers, though it doesn't stop the cold. Icicles grow on everything like glistening, silver fungi. Beards of frost tinsel the bridge and the lookout railings. Most nights I wander the bridge, and my feet crunch on frozen stars. Ice crystals grow and numerate, spreading the wild seeds of winter. It's beautiful in the way that an empty ocean or a lonely moon is.

Not long after we reached the lighthouse, some of my belongings were shipped to me from the orphanage along with a letter from Sister Annika.

Dear Eliana,

We hope you are adjusting well in your new clime. Your warmth is missed here at the Church but you are remembered by the burn marks on the furniture and the smoke stains on the ceilings. Those will cost a pretty penny to repair.

The girls are all doing just fine. Milagros is now completely blind, but it was only a matter of time, really. She is producing more gems than ever before and insisted that we enclose some with your belongings. Marta is pious as ever. She inquires as to your happiness up there in the frozen north. Melusine moons about the window. She complains of dry skin, but this time of year it's to be expected. Flora's wings are now permanently crimson from that almighty divine moment in the chapel. Juniper has recovered nicely since the wedding, and we let her keep that abhorrent bird.

Overall, we thought the wedding went splendidly. The Church has more constituents than ever before. You set off a holy tidal wave of sorts. We are looking to acquire another girl. Someone celestial, but not quite so hot. You were terribly difficult to accommodate, my dear, for all that we loved you anyway.

Give the Prince our best. You are welcome to come back any time for a visit. With enough advance notice we could even arrange a royal tour. God bless.

Love,

Sister Annika

The stones that Milagros sent were in two separate boxes, carefully rolled in cloth. The first box contained the crystals from the spice racks that had hung on the walls of our bedroom. There was the glowing yellow citrine which she cried when I told her the story of my parents, my birth, and my subsequent abandonment. There were gems the color of the ripe fruits she picked from the trees outside her childhood home, and the green rain that she missed so much. There was aquamarine for Melusine's lost oceans and moonstone for Flora's clipped wings. Onyx for Marta's dark stoicism. Rubies for Juniper's bloody secrets. Each jewel represented a moment that had cemented our lives together. I don't know how I never noticed it before. All together, they told the story of our friendship.

The second box was full of unfamiliar gems, infinitely more precious and of higher quality. They were painful, jagged things that burned with intensity. Resting atop them all was the smooth, shimmering blue stone Milagros had shown to Marta and I in the kitchen that morning—her dream tear, which contained all her hopes of love and becoming a princess. I took both boxes to the bridge and heaved them over the railing. They formed a glittering arc of color against the ice-white world as they fell.

That night, after North and I made love, he massaged salve onto my frostbite. Then, as he applied aloe to his own burnt skin, he asked, "Is something wrong?"

My reply was interrupted by a tapping, a pecking sound coming from outside. "What is that?" North asked. He moved to get out of bed, but I stopped him.

"It's nothing," I said. "Just birds, I think."

I wanted to tell him about the boxes of gems, but he was already snoring, puffs of cold air escaping his mouth and turning white in our post-coital steam. I lay in bed, unable to sleep. The numbness was spreading through me again, like it always did after we were together. One day, I feared, I would find myself extinguished.

The next morning North was delighted. Overnight the ice wall had been decorated in Milagros' tears. Gemstones of different colors and sizes arranged in swirling patterns and dazzling displays. Hundreds of birds perched atop the lighthouse: buntings, ptarmigans, ivory gulls, and snow owls. They had salvaged every last crystal Milagros had given me, scoured the frozen waves to return her tears. Maybe it was a gift from the Lord. Maybe it was punishment. North and I differed in our opinions.

Now, each morning, as I cross the slick bridge to the frozen lighthouse, I look out at the story of my past. Some things are clearer looking backward, it's true. Here, at the end of the earth, it is hard to repent.

THE DECLINE OF A PROFESSIONAL MARIONETTE

There are only so many times you can perform *The Nutcracker* before you want to move on. Tedium will cause a girl to do anything, like hop a gypsy wagon headed south and dance for a scattering of coins. I pay my way to England with some clogging, a little yodeling, and a few classical ballet numbers that are mostly lost to folks on the road. No words required. I keep a distance from the other passengers on the wagon. There are lots of shadow puppets on board and they make me nervous. They are a darkly ethereal and hard to understand bunch. Every marionette girl worth her salt has been warned to steer clear of them.

When the wagon stops off for libations, I find myself in the village of Bluebird-Upon-Thames. Something about the place is perfectly enchanting. Wind chimes tinkle across the lazy afternoon and birdsong hangs suspended from crystallized threads of breeze. There is a tiny pub with whitewashed walls, a thatched roof, and hanging baskets filled with brilliant red geraniums. It is called The Lonely Horse Pub.

I have no intention of staying. I only plan to have some sort of ladylike refreshment for the road. A glass of elderberry wine, maybe. However, a fellow named Mauricio approaches me as soon as I walk in the door. He is The Lonely Horse's stage and talent manager.

"How about a job, ducky? A full time position if you're up for it. You have a lively sparkle in your eye."

I've been trained in the Classics, but I can do it all, so being a barmaid is within the realm of possibility. Exciting even, because of its pedestrian nature. I imagine serving refreshments to gentlemen just finishing a game of croquet. I have an outfit perfectly suited for the role: a Norwegian-looking, laced-bodice frock from "The Lonely Goatherd" sequence. It was early in my career and I don't often revisit it.

And braids. I know how to wear braids. I'm told my hair was made to match a Russian princess who used to own me. It isn't made of yarn. It swings when I move and blows around in the breeze. It is long and thick and blond.

I let the wagon move on without me and rent a room above the Lonely Horse for the night. The next morning I speak to Mauricio about the job. As manager of the pub, he slinks about the different rooms, eavesdropping on conversations and chain-smoking cigarettes. He's got one of those oily handlebar mustaches. I bet he's seen his days of tying heroines to train tracks. Now his accent is clipped and British. I think he is trying for an echo of Basil Fawlty.

"We don't get new people around here often," he says.

"I don't mind," I tell him. I give him my most charming smile. "I love your village."

In truth, I do. Bluebird-Upon-Thames is like an antiquated Peter Pan set. I can't wait to see what kind of stories unfold here. All the houses have eaves that shine bright in the summer moonlight. At night the stars swing from the skies like ripe globes waiting to be plucked from their strings. A pristine model of the Thames, untouched by pollution, runs alongside the village. There are dancing bluebells, paper swans, and cherry trees that trickle scented blossoms into the breeze.

"The regulars," says Mauricio. "You have to make a splash with them."

I am confident enough in my own talents. I am beautifully crafted, well trained, and versatile. I paint the blush of English roses onto my smooth cheeks. The braids make me look positively pastoral.

·

On my first shift, Mauricio hangs a sign outside the pub. It says, "Meet Cressida! The Lonely Horse's newest acquisition."

Acquisition doesn't bother me at all. Cressida does. I've had so many names. I've been so many people. Clara, Pamina, Rosalinde, Mabel, Nimue, and many more. The one I feel closest to is Melkorka. She was a mute Viking slave from an Icelandic saga, but I suppose she's not appropriate for this kind of setting. Still, Cressida feels a little overly feminine and flowery.

The bar fills up slowly, then all at once it's packed. The crowd is rough and rowdy. My joints are flexible and limber enough to perform ballets, but I am not equipped to pour pints or make vodka-lemonades. That's the problem when you have fingers with no traction. The swift paced tasks that go along with my new role as a barmaid prevent me from showing off my training in witty banter, demure smiles, and classical dance. I don't have any chance to break out into song.

"Land's sakes!" shouts a salty fellow named Scrimshaw when I drop his glass of Brown Seaman's Stout for the third time. "Where do you come from that you can't carry a pint?"

"Salzburg," I say. They all know that this means the Salzburg Marionette Theatre, famous particularly for *The Nutcracker*, *Die Fledermaus*, and *The Magic Flute*.

A reverent hush carries across the audience of drinkers for a moment. I'm the real deal. However, it only lasts for a moment.

"Ships ahoy," Scrimshaw says. "Then give me a gin and tonic, girl. Just slide it on down the bar. That'll do."

I devise a system of pushing the glasses under the rotating liquor taps and slinging them toward the customers. Though the barmaid that I replaced apparently had flexi-grip hands that allowed her to handle pint glasses with no problem, she has already been forgotten. The men switch their requests to easy-to-handle drinks and the first night is a success.

The owner of the pub is named Hildy. She is Swedish, though she has adapted well to the British countryside. She paints her face with dark eyeliner that slides down her wooden cheeks like tears when she drinks chardonnay. She owns the pub because of a divorce from a rich scoundrel of a husband. He also left behind a daughter, an introverted teenage lamb named Lulu, who tries to hurry Hildy home after too many glasses of wine. Lulu stands on two legs and wears regular clothes and thick reading glasses, but there is no hiding the cotton-white fur covering her body.

Hildy pretends to like me because sales are rocketing. "Watch out for the women," she says. But not many women come into her place. My first acquaintances are all men, the most notable being an Irish marionette named Aengus. He is ruggedly crafted and handsome in a way that rings of green hills and wild oceans. He's married to a Roman gypsy named Zulfinya who belly dances with snakes wrapped around her neck in the village square. They have two little boys who play the tin whistle while she dances. Aengus is a traditionally trained *seanchaí*. He tells stories in Old Irish and shoots fire from his lips after drinking shots of absinthe. He's also a mesmerist, at least that's what the others say. His eyes are blue and gleaming. His artist built entire oceans inside of them.

"Watch out for that one," says Scrimshaw, noticing the long glances I give Aengus. Although Hildy owns the bar and Mauricio runs it, Scrimshaw is the social centerpiece and the gatekeeper of moral turpitude around here. His moods generally direct the other puppets. His actions give them cues. Scrimshaw is a baleen-haired manikin made from the ivory bones of a sperm whale. Bits of him chip off and flake when he gets too animated. He's something to be admired, a real piece of performance history. He's even managed to cultivate a whale-boned beer belly.

Despite his authority, I nearly swoon when Aengus shoots fire. Scrimshaw does his best to keep our interactions at a minimum, but the looks Aengus give me pass right over the old whale's ornate head and leave me wanting to burst into song.

•

The Lonely Horse turns out to be a rich place. Rich in character. There is an Indian magician named Ashok who comes in occasionally with his white monkey, Samosa. There is Johnny Twinkle, a retired Santa Claus marionette. Gary, a dried-out husk of a crocodile with a toothless grin and black pellet eyes. And a pair of gin-blossomed musicians named Rootabaga and McBoozle who play out-of-tune renditions of "God Save the Queen" and "Rule Britannia." Every so often a beautiful witch who dances professionally in a shadow puppet pub on the other side of town comes in for a glass of elderberry wine. She comes in through the back door, usually when nobody is about, leaving sparkles and mystery in her wake. There are so many different characters it's overwhelming. The only thing missing is a plot.

Scrimshaw says as much one afternoon while I'm polishing the beer taps. "Something's been missing around here for a while."

I have been trying to convince Hildy and Mauricio that we need more musical numbers in the pub. Or choreographed dance routines. I know *Swan Lake*, *The Nutcracker*, even *Cats* if we wanted to get a little avant-garde. It is hard to imagine Scrimshaw bending his old bones to classical numbers, but we could do it. It's what we need.

"Not music," Scrimshaw says, dark-and-stormy froth gathering around his clattering jawbones. "Plot, girl. We need plot. Something's got to happen."

"Hmmm," I say. "Someone goes on a journey."

"Ridiculous," says Scrimshaw. "Been done a thousand times!"

"Love," I try.

He looks disdainful.

"Betrayal," I suggest.

He snorts. "Happens every day."

I shrug my shoulders and sigh.

"Don't you," he says, seeing the look on my face. "Don't you dare start one of your fancy musical numbers. This isn't Cinderella."

Off in the corner Mauricio twirls his mustache. Rootabaga and McBoozle are engaged in a loud debate about whether or not the Scots are truly indebted to the Queen. Ashok is reading a book while Samosa steals peanuts off the bar and chatters to Gary, who is pretending to be asleep. Hildy is on her third glass of wine. Aengus is staring at me with gleaming glass eyes the color of endless oceans.

•

When I am not working at the Lonely Horse I like to walk along the river. Oftentimes I see the dancing witch feeding the swans. In my own experience, they are surprisingly bad tempered for paper birds, but they eat out of her hands like pets. Some days I trace the path of the gypsy wagon that brought me here. Some days I count bluebirds and pick wildflowers. Sometimes I practice at smoking cigarettes. I use dish soap and a wand to capture the smoke, and watch it swirl around inside the bubbles until they burst into mini grenades.

Occasionally I take Lulu on walks while Hildy works. An adolescent sheep needs as many allies as she can have. Over the years I've played many roles, including a shepherdess, so I try to use my experience to help Lulu.

"I wish I were you, Cressida," she bleats, clambering along the river path. "You have no idea how the other teeeease me!"

Lulu and I work on enunciation and clipping her vowels. There is not much I can do about her fur. If we shave her, she will be pink and naked. Instead, I help curl her eyelashes and teach her to talk with a French accent.

"Don't bleat," I tell her.

She nods, but her big lamb eyes well up with tears. Bleating is part of her nature.

One day Aengus cuts us off at the edge of the river. It is to be expected. Predictable. I can't imagine what purpose he was made for if not to seduce women.

Lulu leaps off startled into the bushes and we are left standing alone beside the eddying Thames. Swans slide over the gleaming waters gracefully.

"Well, here we are," Aengus says, giving me a charming half-smile.

I raise an eyebrow, although it is already perfectly arched. I try to think of an appropriate song to sing but none come to mind. I am about to continue on my way when he grabs my arm.

"Cressida," he says, the words like waves on an ocean. His whirlpool eyes latch on to mine.

Over the years I've learned to be wary of clichés. For goodness' sake, *Die Fledermaus*. If I have learned anything about adultery, jealousy, and scorned lovers, I learned it from that play. I will not be the new barmaid who falls for the handsome, married mesmerist.

I shake my arm free. Around us the trees are raining cherry blossoms. My blond hair tumbles in the breeze and whispers across my shoulders. Everything is seductive.

"I thought we could talk alone," he says.

"No." I shake my head.

His eyes are blue like the sky and the water. He is about to tell me a story, but just as the words are ready to tumble out of his mouth, a bevy of paper swans skid out of the water in a frightened murmuration. There is a rippling in the river. A crocodile head emerges, followed by a mangled body of half-shorn scales and peeling skin..

"Nice day," says Gary, plopping himself down in the tender sun.

I have never been so relieved to see a crocodile.

•

Aengus has mesmerized me. I should have never looked into his eyes. Now, every time the door swings open I expect him to walk into The Lonely Horse. Every night I listen for his Irish lilt to come whispering through the pub. When I see his wife belly dancing in the town square, I decide she is ugly and old. Made of cheap wood. What kind of name is Zulfinya? Common. She's probably only ever been used for street performances or folk plays. His kids make my stomach turn upside down with envy.

I tell myself "no" a thousand times. A million. I avoid the river. Nothing works.

"You're not yourself, Cressida," Scrimshaw says. He's noticed the way I've been mooning about aimlessly. Disappointment radiates from his deep sea bones.

In truth, I am confused about who "myself" is. I have been too many characters for too long. I've seen it happen before. The decline of a professional marionette.

"Another love story." Scrimshaw shakes his head. "I thought you were going to give us something new."

But I'm only a puppet. I try to hold myself apart from ubiquitous plots or obvious Greek allegories, but it is a constant struggle. I am weary of watching Hildy and Mauricio and the rest of them, night after night, reenacting the same plays. Bluebird-Upon-Thames proceeds on its lonely and predictable continuum.

•

On my night off, I go into the bar down the road. The nameless shadow puppet pub that all of the other marionettes avoid. I want to make something happen. The first person I see is the dancing witch. Shadows surround her, but she is perfectly at ease with their presence. She smells like sweet dark things, night blooming jasmine and fireflies in cool meadows. Her body is made of something smooth and dark and diaphanous. She flashes me a knowing smile.

"What brings you here, Cressida?"

The shadows lean toward us, waiting for my answer. I just want something. Something different. But I say, "I don't know why I'm here."

"Write down your wish on this piece of paper. Set it on fire and throw it up into the sky," she whispers.

I can't do that. My hair is synthetic. I'm made of wood. I never go anywhere near open flames. Instead, I watch the sad and seductive silhouettes of shadow puppets while I drink ginger brandy. They act out exotic dramas that I have never seen before. Never imagined before. They are fluid. Motion. Freedom. My body, with its joints and solidity, seems cumbersome and unwieldy.

The dancing witch brings more glasses of fiery liquid that scalds my throat and sets my heart on fire. I imagine I hear Scrimshaw's voice faraway on the moonlit breeze. He is calling my name like a sad sea shanty. But it is nighttime. The air is enchanted with moons and stars. I drink some more. The dancing witch showers me in paper peacock feathers that fall to the floor, matching her sinuous movements.

As the evening unwinds, it barrels on towards a thrilling wrongness. Aengus shows up. Of course he does. If I had followed the witch's instructions this would have been the result. He would be the result. He sits down beside me and the witch freshens our drinks.

"Well, here we are," he whispers into my ear. And then the words come. Mysterious and powerful in a language I can't understand. All lit up with the green fire of absinthe and desire.

And then things unravel. Or maybe they come to an inevitable conclusion. It must be the work of some mad puppeteers. Nothing in any of my former lives has prepared me for what comes next.

•

I don't remember bringing Aengus back to the room above the Lonely Horse, only vague recollections of vulgar puppetry. In the morning the sun shines bright through the windows, wrapping us in lemon cellophane. I push him off of me before he can speak and he clatters to the ground. He has a gypsy wife and kids who are somewhere waiting for him.

This is the beginning of my troubles in Bluebird-Upon-Thames. Hildy does not want me to take her daughter on walks anymore. The women start calling in now. Bold and unafraid. I was something before I slipped up. Now it doesn't matter if I am made of the finest linden. It doesn't matter if I have had the starring roles in Salzburg. I'm a marionette with loose morals. A common floozy. The hanging baskets of geraniums swing back and forth with the whip-slams of the pub door. My joints are jittery. I drop a bottle of champagne that a few of the village ladies are having with their lunches and they shriek at me, clipped British accents and accusatory glares.

"Well," I say to Hildy. "Lots of new business now."

She looks at me with slippery eyes and doesn't respond. Mauricio shakes his head and twirls his mustache, eavesdropping in the corners.

In the evenings, the women return home to take care of the children and the men reclaim their usual positions at the bar. I am not one for stage fright, but this is a different feeling. Being watched without being adored.

Rootabaga and McBoozle look depressed. Gary won't meet my gaze. It's terrible.

"Lunch tomorrow," Scrimshaw says. "My place. I think we should have a talk."

I can only nod at his whale-boned skull. I am grateful for any kindness I can get.

Aengus doesn't come in at all.

•

Birds are always singing here, but today they are quiet, perhaps because they sense me coming down the wilted bluebell path. I pick a few flowers for Scrimshaw and stick them in an old bottle I find at the edge of the river.

"Really, Cressida," he says, ushering me into his house. Nautical maps hang on the walls. I can hear the distant ocean roaring from the row of conch shells lining his window. "Have a seat, girl. Drink some tea. You have landed yourself in a horrendous heap of trouble."

Maybe because Scrimshaw used to be a whale, he manages to cut straight through the niceties. "You're not the first," he says briskly. "There was a girl before you and a girl before her."

This stabs at me terribly. "You mean with Aengus."

"Sure," says Scrimshaw. "Disaster every time." He looks disappointed. "You'll have to leave, of course."

"I have to leave?" I say. "Why do I have to leave?"

He heaves his shoulders. It is like watching a sea beast navigate rough waves. "That's the way it goes here. Same every time. We don't deviate from the script."

If I could cry, this would bring tears to my eyes. I can't help but feel tricked.

"I hate to see you go, Cressida. We've become fond of you."

It is impossible to speak.

"Here's the thing," says Scrimshaw. "If you stay, the women will torment you. You've got no place amongst the good people of Bluebird-Upon-Thames now. There's nothing for it. You're going to become a shadow."

In truth, I already feel less substantial. "You knew this would happen," I say.

Scrimshaw shrugs. "We were hoping you'd be different. Deliver us something new."

I square up my shoulders. I try to summon the strength of the Viking slave Melkorka. "And you," I say. "You're just a side note in a provincial tragedy."

He looks apologetic, but he stirs his tea and doesn't say a word.

•

During my farewell shift at the Lonely Horse the mood is gloomy. Rootabaga blows his nose into McBoozle's coat. Their eyes are red and teary. Gary and Scrimshaw sit quietly, playing a somber game of spades in the corner. Hildy and Mauricio are at a table in the back crunching numbers and discussing who is going to cover my shifts.

"You could stick it out, Cressida," cries Rootabaga. "Eventually things will calm down."

I consider it for a moment, though we both know that's not true. I'm no good at improvisation.

When Aengus walks in the whole place goes silent. All eyes are on us.

"So," he says.

I ignore him. I ignore his lopsided smile. I'd like to lay my hands on the rat bastard who created him.

"There are some things that we should discuss," he says.

I try to glare, but I'm not sure I'm able to. I was meant for fairytales, operas, and happy endings.

"I'm leaving tomorrow," I tell him. "There is nothing to talk about."

I don't look into those glass eyes of his. Instead, I think of the marionettes who came before me and sank down into their depths. Shadows, Scrimshaw had said, all of them.

Just then Hildy knocks over her glass of chardonnay. Here come the tears. As she dabs at her blouse she starts wailing.

Mauricio hands her a dishtowel and lights two cigarettes. One for each of them. Hildy snuffles like an indignant child.

"You're different," says Aengus. Rip curls. A voice full of honey. It's like he knows what I'm thinking. Or maybe what I want to hear. "Not like the others."

I *am* different. I want to believe that. Perhaps Scrimshaw was wrong. What do whales know of love anyway? I can replace Zulfinya. Get my own thatched house with geraniums. Learn to love spending my days walking beside the paper swans.

I see Aengus's lips are moving.

Have children. I'm a fine age to settle down and have a few puppets of my own.

A loud honking noise disrupts the pub. Rootabaga and McBoozle are strategically testing out a pair of moth-eaten bagpipes beside us.

Nothing else matters. Aengus's eyes are on mine.

A little girl. With limbs of linden and wild Irish curls.

I feel his breath but I can't hear his words.

"Land ho!" Scrimshaw bellows. Beside him Lulu is doing cartwheels and back handsprings to get my attention.

"Cressida," Aengus says, drawing me closer, and my name sounds perfect now. Like endless waves on an ocean. "Cressida."

I turn away from him and hold my hands over my ears.

The witch is smiling at me, standing at the back door right on cue.

•

Sometimes a girl wants to go back to predictable plots. Sometimes a girl wants scripts, and audiences beyond sheep and paper swans. Cherry blossoms. Any good puppeteer can make cherry blossoms rain down over a pastoral setting.

When another gypsy wagon passes by, I hop aboard and dance for a scattering of coins. It's the same as before, except this time I don't ignore the shadows. While the wagon travels, I tell the shadow puppets stories about the marionettes I left behind, the paper swans and dancing bluebells. They hover around me, thirsty for color and character. They don't talk much, but they are an emotional bunch.

After a while, the freshness of the pain begins to go away and the vibrancy of Bluebird-Upon-Thames fades from my memory. I no longer remember the ocean color of Aengus's eyes. I forget the tattooed designs carved on Scrimshaw's arms and legs. I let the shadow puppets absorb my memories until I am new again.

When the wagon stops off for fun and libations, I find myself in a village called Land's End. It is nestled among white sand cliffs beside a sweeping sea. Beyond the brightly colored market streets and the marina filled with sparrows and singing sailors, there are starfish and humpback whales and coquettish mermaids. Perhaps I could try my hand at being a fishmonger. Or a piratesse. Surely there is room for a yodeling, ballet dancing, opera singing, classically-trained marionette from Salzburg. It is a perfectly enchanting place. There is something in the ocean that pulls at my memory, but it is gone just as soon as it's there.

THINKING LIKE A HOG DEER IN THE HIMALAYAS

We sleep in identical quilt-covered beds while the mountains creak and groan outside the walls and the wind dusts the rooftop with the music of snowflakes and falling stars. In the freezing dark of our first winter together, our wings solidify and grow, their fragile transparent tissue thickens and turns rubbery, making us slow and awkward, our movements as sticky and uncertain as glue. During this first phase of new growth we are crepuscular, existing between dark and light. We sleep in heavy, deathlike trances and only venture outside during the gloaming or when the moon is full. In the beginning, I am sedated in order to keep from leaving the school. I gnash my teeth between wing-growing spasms. Despite the air of uniformity, I hold myself separate from the rest of the girls.

Rani is our teacher and our surrogate mother. She does her best to make us comfortable while we undergo our transformations. The dim warmth of the boarding house cocoons us against the Himalayan winter. The air is perfumed with smoky incense haze. Piles of grouse-down pillows litter the polished floors in case we are stricken with exhaustion while walking to and from the common area and our shared bedrooms. We suffer growing pains and homesickness in synchronized waves.

In the beginning there are seven of us. However, while we are still drowsy with transformation, the most disoriented moth girl wanders off and disappears into a blizzard. Rani assures us she has likely been taken in by friendly Sherpas, but we suspect the paralysis of sudden avalanches, or the deadly silence of prowling snow leopards. Becoming a moth girl is fraught with its own brand of peril.

To pass the time, we learn celestial navigation by candlelight. We chart and explore the dim boarding house, misgauging distances and bumping into things. Many of us bruise. Some of us scar. For the longest time we are so easily bent and dented that it is hard to imagine anything else. And then, almost overnight, our new appendages become strong and supple and covered in soft fur. The group mentality fractures as the corners of Rani's house glow with piles of moon-white dander.

"I know this is yours, Gurdeep," Rani says, toeing a copper-colored fluff ball toward me. She smiles like she is making a joke out of it. As if to say: *molting is something that unites us.*

It does no such thing. Rani's smile doesn't dull the savage scorn of the other moth girls. They avert their eyes. They want no part of my personal disgrace. My face prickles with humiliation. I pick up my wing lint quickly and stuff it into my pocket. The first molting is always the worst. Fur and hormones all over the place. Try as we might, there is no dignified way to groom. This is what Rani tells us, anyway.

"Relax," Rani says. She touches my shoulder so close to my new wings that I jump. "Be proud of it. It sets you apart and makes you an individual. *Embrace* it."

Her outpouring of motherly moth-woman advice makes the other girls giggle and ensures that I will be teased for the rest of the day. Even worse, it makes me miss my own mother. She and Rani were in flight school together as girls. My mother didn't tell me much about those days, but she spoke of Rani as a friend. I try to picture Rani as a young girl rather than my teacher, but I can't.

"*Embrace* yourself, Gurdeep," Shobha says with a snicker. "No one else ever will."

Shobha has quickly become the bully of our pack. She elbows Pomegranate in the ribs and they both crease forward into wild laughter. I could point out the several wispy tufts of silver-green that float down to the floor from their movements, but I don't. I am too much of a lady.

•

By the time the sun rears up over the ice fields in early spring, we are different creatures entirely. Our wings are strong, lightweight, whiskered propellers. They purr and vibrate against our spines. Shobha looks truly terrifying, her hair bleached white by the thin Himalayan nights. Her skin glows. Her black eyes glitter. Pomegranate's hair used to be an awkward ginger color. Now her tangled curls are a sugary shock of pink and magenta that is obscene against the frozen landscape. She exudes a terrible wantonness that worries Rani and awes the rest of us. The Sherpas follow her around like hypnotized animals.

The other girls have made similar transformations. Daya and Deva, twin sisters who speak to each other in serpentine whispers, have become icy, mountain wraiths. Their hair coils out from their cold faces in frozen corkscrews. Their fingers and toes are pale purple. They smell like the sky and eat popsicles made of marmalade.

Candle is less intimidating than the others. Her eyes have

turned the color of honey. Her wings practically drip with the sticky shade. She is a distant cousin of Rani's, which makes her act superior, and she is quick to rat us out for any minor moth-girl infractions. She spends the days gazing at herself in a mirror above her bed and only comes outside for the required flight training regiments.

I try hard not to glimpse my own reflection in the frosted glass of the windows. I am the only one having some heartsickness over losing my former self. The others shiver and shine and shriek like mountain banshees. "Yip! Yip! Yip!" The moth girls' voices bounce off the glaciers and crack the clear ice near the edge of the stream.

We are practicing wind-running today. Icy swells run down off the snowcaps and ripple the air in giant blasts that gasp for the sea. Our wings spread out from their cramped crouches to taste the evergreen breath of the mountains. Our feet pound the ice and snow trying to keep up, combining ancient rhythms with familiar ones. Rani has forbidden us to be completely airborne yet. We are still in the fledgling stage.

"There is nothing worse than premature flight," she tells us. There is such vehemence in her voice when she says this that we all believe her. Even Shobha follows directions with a discreet roll of her eyes.

Contrary to popular belief, flying is not something that comes naturally to moth girls. It takes lots of practice before you attempt the real deal. Throughout the winter we studied aeronautics and memorized stellar navigation co-ordinates. Now Rani leads us in simulated flight patterns. We buzz beneath the frozen sun, our feet trilling across the ground, the wind filling our heads with freedom and frozen promises. The other girls practice restraint to keep from taking off.

Me, I am quite the opposite. I don't like heights. I hate the altitude. The thin air makes me dizzy. My sky-bound destiny keeps me awake most nights and torments me throughout the day. I never run out of things to worry about. There are all kinds of dangers to real flight: downdrafts, blizzards, frostbite, disorientation, snow blindness, and wing freeze. I click them off in my head like a recording as I run. It causes my feet to stick to the ground. It makes my breath wheeze and sputter. I carry onions in both pockets for moments like these. The fleshy aroma restores my equilibrium and replaces the ground beneath my feet. It is an old trick. One that Rani told me about. I try to draw on the strength of ancient moth girls who may have been more like myself. Girls who relied on totems to channel the solid strength of the earth.

"Gurdeep is holding us back," Shobha says when we stop for a break. She is panting lightly. She very nearly touched a cloud today—its tendrils are impaled on her icicle-spiked hair. As soon as she points this out, six pairs of glowing, slanted eyes turn toward me. I drop the onion that I'm holding up to my nose. The rest of the group looks disgusted.

"Some people don't deserve wings," Pomegranate mutters.

"Some people didn't ask for wings," I say, but the girls turn away in unison and move off again.

Most of the girls are from around here. Shobha was born on a nearby mountain. Pomegranate was raised in a grey city that curves alongside the Ganges River. Daya and Deva are from Kathmandu. Even Candle grew up among ice and snow. They have spent their lives preparing for the moment they would grow wings and receive their training.

I am different. I was born in the Sundarbans, the ocean forest. I was raised among the salted roots of the mangroves and the gentle swells of the sea. My mother fled these mountains when she was my age. The only part of the story I ever knew was the shape of the cauterized scars on her back. Wingless, she delivered me into a world that was hot and poisonous and slow. Back home, I knew how to watch out for the strong jaws of the water monitor, the low growl of a hungry Bengalese tiger, or the knobby hide of a crocodile's back. Here, everything that is beautiful is dangerous.

•

After the other moth girls booby trap my flight pack with a rotten banana, demagnetize my compass, and shave patches of fur off my wings while I am sleeping, Rani pulls me aside for a chat.

"Listen, Gurdeep," she says, her smooth skin furrowed with concern. "I know you are not adjusting here. Tell me if there's anything I can do to help you along and I will do it. I hate to see any of my girls having such a tough time."

"Send me home," I tell her. Home is where I belong. I miss the memory of my mother. In the Sundarbans I could feel her everywhere. In the salty breeze off the ocean. In the warm rains and the gentle tapping of the mangrove leaves. We used to collect the sweet fruits of the nipa palm, harvesting the feathery leaves to weave baskets and patch weak spots in the thatching of our hut. Sometimes we brewed *bahal* from the sap, a drink that I was never allowed to partake in, but that the people of the nearby villages would consume as fast as we could produce it. It was another one of mother's secrets, like her life before the Sundarbans.

"I'm done molting now," I tell Rani, thrusting my chin up stubbornly. "The worst of it is over, right? I don't even want to fly. Please let me go home."

I can see by the tears swelling behind the polished black of her pupils that this is not going to happen. "You belong here," she says. "Moth girls belong to the snow-cold moon. They belong to the ice and the sky. It is a part of your destiny."

"My mother left," I say.

"Your mother tried to escape her place in the world," she says. "It never works that way. Moth girls belong to the mountains."

I feel the mangrove forests receding from me as she says this. I feel the cold erasing memories of my mother. My veins turn to threads of icy tinsel. Rani's face is sad but impassive. She touches my wings and then touches her own.

"This is your new family. This is your new home."

I nod, but refuse to accept her words. There must be some kind of way out.

•

Pomegranate is having a lusty affair with a Sherpa. This is strictly forbidden. Moth girls are to stay celibate for the duration of flight school. Rani says our new identities are too fragile, our concentration too important for carnal distractions. The Sherpas pose a constant threat with their sinewy climbing muscles and almond eyes. They watch us with something akin to reverence as they build our landing platforms and mark the white mountaintops with flight-pattern flags. They call us the *Astomi*, the apple smellers. They believe we are an ancient race of mythological monsters, not a pack of adolescent girls.

Pomegranate's Sherpa is from the village of Pangboche. Whenever he visits, the frosted air fills with the scent of old mysteries and conifers. He looks at Pomegranate as if she is a goddess or a beast, and in his gaze she grows bigger than the horizon.

"Ang says I am more beautiful than the sun," she brags as she combs out her curls before supper.

The other girls listen with a combination of envy and anger. We would all like a Sherpa, but we don't dare face Rani's wrath. "Moth girls don't need Sherpas," Rani is fond of saying. "Soon you will be able to fly. Don't make ties to the ground."

Rani has a bum wing. That's how she got stuck here with us rather than becoming the goddess of her own mountain range somewhere. She makes a wonderful teacher, but the look in her eyes as our feet begin to lift off the ground is more painful than windburn. Sometimes I fantasize about tearing off my own wings and stitching them to Rani's back so she can fly me home. In my fantasies, Rani flies like she is made of fire. She swoops and dives and glides and somersaults before returning me to my marshes, where my mother waits at the edge of the ocean forest surrounded by hog deer and smiling crocodiles.

"Come on, Gurdeep," Rani says after a particularly grueling flight practice. "Why are you so stuck to the ground?"

"I am a hog deer," I tell her.

She gives me a questioning look. There are no hog deer in the Himalayas. There are only snow leopards and the occasional wandering yak.

"They are little things that bark and run like heavy pigs," I tell her. "They duck under branches and high roots rather than soaring over them like other deer."

"There are no hog deer here," she says dismissively.

Of course I know this. Hog deer belong in the Sundarbans. They have adapted to their environment perfectly in order to survive among the world's deadliest predators. Back home they are an example of competitive evolution. They care nothing for beauty or gracefulness. Up here, in the snow covered stillness, they would be as out of place as I am.

"Hog deer are survivors," I hear my mother's voice saying. I remember crouching behind a log and watching a small faun snuffling in the damp moss, dangerously close to a green whip snake. My mother held me back to restrain me from interfering, and almost immediately a mature hog deer with heavy teats emerged, trampling the whip snake to death with her delicately pointed hooves.

A hog deer would never stay here. A hog deer would find its way home. But I am helpless in this habitat. I need an ally. Someone who understands this world.

•

In order to talk to Ang I have to catch him away from Rani and the rest of the girls. I tell myself that it is only for survival's sake and try not to acknowledge the petty thrill the idea gives me. I don't relish the thought of Pomegranate's rage if she discovers I am trying to steal her man.

The Sherpas camp together in a clearing of snow-covered huts. They are the only men who can breathe the air this high in the mountains. Over many generations, their bodies have adapted to the altitude. They are a funny mix of mountains and ground. They speak in old languages peppered with new. They wear traditional woolen bakhus and bright thermal jackets. They worship us. We are a part of their mountain religion.

While the other Sherpas keep warm in huddled groups around fire pits with mugs of chang and instant coffee, Ang prays alone at a makeshift gompa. His bakhu is somber and he wears an embroidered cap lined with yak fur. I watch from behind a large snowdrift. His prayers make my wings flutter.

After weeks of spying with no results, I finally decide to fake an illness in order to be left alone in the boarding house. Rani takes the other girls out on an all-day flight expedition and they leave me behind. Shobha and Pomegranate are particularly delighted.

"Try not to bore yourself to death while we're gone," Pomegranate says, dissolving any guilt I was feeling.

After they leave, I strut around the empty boarding house, rifling through the girls' belongings and speaking to myself in confident tones. "I am a temptress. I am a mountain goddess." I force myself over to the mirror by Candle's bed. I prepare myself for a shock. I hold my breath, still my thoughts, and look square in the face of it.

I have changed.

Black eyes and black hair. Eyebrows like arrows. I have no more baby face, only a wild, sorrowful look. Skin the color of salted mangroves. My wings are spotted ochre. They shimmer in the fading sunlight, dusting the air with miniature prisms.

I think of the hog deer to regain my composure. They are unflappable and small and strong. I pull an onion out of my pocket and sniff greedily. I pull Candle's makeup palette out from under her bed and with a steady hand I draw exotic shades of experience and mystery on my face.

•

Ang doesn't hear me approaching. I flap my wings while he is lost in prayer and snowflakes swirl around his face. I am the first thing he sees when he opens his eyes.

"Lhamo," he says in a reverent voice. "Goddess."

I don't correct him.

"I need your help," I say. I try to look commanding. "You must help me escape."

He looks confused. "Escape from what? You are a goddess of the mountains."

"I need to get back to the Sundarbans," I say. "If you help me, I will give you anything you want."

His eyes swell at the mention of that word. *Anything.* Snowfall dusts the smooth prayer stones of his gompa. I know from the way he kneels that there is something he wants.

"Anything?"

I nod. "But you have to get me out of here. And you can't tell any of the other girls."

High-pitched yips rise up over the mountain pass and we both flinch.

"Will you help me?" I ask.

Ang locks eyes with me. "I am loyal to Pomegranate. I don't want to anger her."

I shrug. "If you don't help me, I will tell Rani about you. Pomegranate will be thrown out of flight school. Then you will anger *all* of the Astomi. If you help me, no one has to know anything. We will keep each other's secrets."

Ang's face pales. The snow swirls. Another Sherpa calls out from close by and Ang jumps to his feet as I retreat back into the swirling snow.

"I'll be waiting for you," I tell him.

He doesn't answer.

•

A week passes before he comes to find me. One night I am lying in bed scratching at my wings and thinking of crocodiles when I smell Pangboche on the breeze. Ang is waiting at the window.

"I thought you'd never come," I say.

He grimaces in the moonlight. "We have to be quick. My father is dying."

I leave behind a note to Rani that says not to search for me. It thanks her for her kindness and attempts to explain my unhappiness. I mention my mother, her scarred back, hoping Rani will understand.

I follow Ang out into the cold. *Crunch. Crunch.* Boots over snow. *Flutter. Flutter.* My wings strain for autonomy from my shoulders. My toes skim the soft snowdrifts. My footprints are no more than a suggestion beside Ang's heavy bootstep. He leads me carefully down the side of the mountain, walking like a grief-stricken goat. He says nothing and the moonlight fills in his silence.

The sun is rising when we reach Pangboche. It is my first time ever in a Sherpa village, and Pangboche is the oldest. It contains secrets and mysteries that only the mountains know. We walk through forests of birch and rhododendron. We pass potato patches, curling rivers, grazing yaks, and houses built into the sides of the mountain.

Ang's face is still tight. We approach a small house with a butter lamp burning on the doorstep. The smell of sickness comes from within. "He needs you now," he says, picking up the lantern. "Come on. It is time for you to do your magic."

I follow him in, my heart thudding in my chest. His father lies beside piles of turnips and dried yak dung. Ang throws some wood on the fire, feeding the flames with hot hopes and ancient prayers.

"Here is the Astomi," he says.

The old man's yellow eyes turn toward me. "Astomi," he whispers. The Sundarbans seem small compared to this dying father.

"Do something," Ang urges.

My wings begin to stir.

"Ang," rasps the old man. "Leave us alone."

Ang stares at us both for a moment before shuffling outside. I am weak with the responsibility that has fallen on my shoulders.

"So," he says. "You have come to find out about your mother."

My mother's image floats before me. Beautiful and sad and strong. In the Sundarbans they called her a witch. Her life was solitary, except for me and the marsh animals. I see no connection between her and a dying Sherpa. "No," I say. "I came to help Ang. In return he will help me go home."

It is hard to recognize any expression in the bed of wrinkles that is the old man's face. There may be sorrow or surprise. I can't tell.

"My son's name is Pasang," he says. "He was born on a Friday. Ang is the name that you Astomi give to all the Sherpas. Your mother called me Ang."

I feel confused. Tricked. Trapped. "How do you know my mother?"

"I see her in your features," he says. His face wrinkles into a thirsty smile. "She was very beautiful. I was already married to Pasang's mother, but I still noticed how beautiful she was."

My wings are now flapping of their own accord. They pound at the air with a pattern I have never felt before. The wailing of a secret wind.

"Who is your father?" he asks me. His voice is papery.

In the Sundarbans, most of the animals exist in groups of mother and child. Anything else is too precarious and unsteady to be trusted. Even the hog deer forgo their normal species mode of herd survival and live in pairs of two. "He is a Sundarban chieftain," I say.

"It was such a long time ago." He sighs like he has stored up that sentence forever.

I square myself up against him, even in his weakened state. "My mother had one love and that is me," I say. "She did not cut off her wings for some old, married Sherpa."

"Maybe not," he says.

We stare at each other for what could be hours. His eyes tell me a story. I see my mother, young and unafraid and powerful. I fill in the spaces that led her to the dangerous sanctuary of the ocean forest.

"Were you there when she did it?" I ask. My skin is scalding hot and my wings do their best to keep me cool.

"She killed my wife," he says. "I had a son to raise with no mother."

"You stink of death and lies," I say. I call for Ang. I try to go outside but the old man thrashes about on his mattress. My wings are still flapping and the ripples from their motion seem to soothe him.

Now Ang is at my side. "Please," Ang says, touching my arm. "Please help him."

I don't do it for the dying man. I do it for his son. My mother would have never given up her wings for a man.

I let fury fuel my flapping. The fire blazes to life, washing us all with warmth. Ang's hair blows back from his face, and I feel my own hair swirling in a cloud above me. My wings fill the room. The old man smiles and Ang's expression smoothes into something recognizable. I see my mother when she was my age, standing in this very place. I see Rani with her limp wing. I'm growing weak and lightheaded, so I reach for my onions, but they're not there. I left with Ang in such a hurry I must have forgotten to pack them. Ang catches me just as

I crumple to the ground and lose consciousness.

·

When I wake up Ang is brewing Sherpa tea in a wooden churn with salt and melted yak butter. He pushes a mug in front of me. It smells like old hiking boots.

"He passed in the night," Ang says. He is not angry with me. In fact, he seems relieved. Lighter somehow.

"I'm sorry," I say, more for Ang's loss than anything else.

He smiles at me with small, chipped teeth. His face creases like oiled animal hide. "You helped him," he says. "My father had renounced the mountain spirits when my mother died in an avalanche. You took away his fear."

"What will you do with him? It must be too cold for a burial."

"Tradition says he will remain in the house for some time. That is how the spirit likes it."

I nod.

"But I haven't forgotten my promise to you," he says.

I watch Ang closely as he waves burning juniper wands through the small space to dispel the death smell. He is sharp and slanted. His body is pure muscle, compact and efficient. He is pulled in close to himself. I suppose there is something of the hog deer in him.

"What makes you like Pomegranate, anyway?" I ask.

Ang shrugs. "She picked me. I don't know. She is Astomi. And she's not like you."

"Like how?"

He shrugs again.

I leave him with his juniper wands and go outside where the snow has fallen fresh and clean. The air is ripe with the scent of conifers and shivering yaks. Ang follows me outside with a mug of tea.

"Your wings have changed," he says, and he's right. The initial spotted ochre pattern has faded and my wings are pure moon white now. Dazzling. I don't have to imagine myself as a goddess anymore.

I sniff the breeze for some indication of what to do. "I don't need your help anymore."

He looks crestfallen and relieved. "Will you return to the Astomi?"

"I haven't decided," I tell him. In truth, I haven't. My homing sense is utterly disoriented. Something else has taken its place. Something that is bigger than my mother, or Ang's father, or flight school.

"You can stay here for a while if you like," Ang says. "Pangboche is good at keeping the mountain's secrets."

But already my wings are flapping. This pattern is different from any I have felt before. Every muscle in my body strains as they open out to their full breadth and thwack at the sky with an ancient and powerful rhythm, knocking Ang into a drift of powdery snow. I forget all of my training immediately and listen to my instincts as my wings get their first breath of mountain air, and I launch into full flight.

Sometimes, nearby villagers would see my mother for advice or good luck, or a particular ailment that couldn't be fixed by their local healers. She always sent them away with too much information. Things they didn't want to hear. Things they couldn't unhear. When she died, there were very few who mourned her. She was killed by a man-eater. A Bengalese tiger. She is buried in the driest part of the ocean forest, where the sea meets the mangrove trees, her grave marked with the hoof prints of stubborn hog deer. Her wings are buried somewhere far apart from her.

SWAMP FOOD AT THE RAPTURE CAFE

On Gospel Sundays, the members of the Blackwater Quartet and Choir gather in Mama Moon's Rapture Café and sing for Jesus while I serve them breakfast. They carol like angels. They croon like golden-throated birds. Their celestial music floods the air and mixes with the scent of bacon and grits, stewed tomatoes, swamp cabbage, and catfish fritters. Conjoined arms, scaled hands, and lobster claws rise up in unison toward our Savior. It makes my heart swell with love and break with loneliness. Sometimes my eyes spill over a little while I serve the main course.

"Food," Mama Moon says, "is the mana of Heaven. It nourishes the heart and replenishes the soul. You are an important part of this, Gabrielle. You give us sustenance."

This is a generous description for a prep cook and waitress. Last summer I applied to the Blackwater Shape Singing School, but the truth of it is, I can't carry a tune. Still, the freaks let me stay on here, even though I have no musical talent whatsoever and have yet to be saved. Mama Moon took me in and put me to work in the kitchen. The cooking itself is rather tedious, but the reward is a front row ticket to the most blissful and heavenly musical performances. The hardest part is carrying out the plates without spilling while tottering at the brink of my own spiritual salvation.

I usually try to serve breakfast just as Percival, the wolf-boy, is crescendo-ing. Sometimes it's hard to tell when he's getting ready to hit his peak, but there is no mistaking it when it happens. The air trembles, the ground quakes, and the cypress trees rain down birds' nests and Spanish moss. In addition to being covered in fur, all hypertrichosics have beautiful voices, a byproduct of the excessive hormones. Percival's voice rings out in such sweet and soulful earnestness that it is all I can do not to fall to my knees and pray. I want to repent, repent, repent. I want to throw myself upon the mercy of divine harmony. Even Horace, the lobster boy, claps his clawed hands in honest ecstasy.

I am not the only one competing for Percival's adoration. Daisy and Buttercup, the prettiest pair of conjoined twins, flutter their lashes and dab at their pale temples with perfumed hankies, looking faint as Percival transforms the entire congregation of freaks and followers into whole-hearted believers, scrubbed clean and kept spotless from sin. "Praise Jesus," they murmur in unison.

But the freaks just want food from me, and their tastes are eclectic. In the case of the Giant, this taste is for mudfish, and lots of it. Mudfish live in the muckiest bits of the swamp and crawl from one puddle to the next, pulling themselves along with strong, flat fins. Filling the Giant's belly takes a half-dozen on a good day. I believe he likes them because they suit his artistic sensibilities. I have overheard him remark on how they persevere enough to survive in a waterless world.

Other foods are not so difficult to catch or prepare, but more grisly to watch being consumed. Clarence and Coriander, the alligator twins, like steamed catfish with the bones intact. They sit side by side, their lidless eyes moist with exertion, and eat the fish like they are playing harmonicas, spitting out bits of vertebrae as they chew. They always clean their plates and wait for seconds before I'm done serving the first course. Mama Moon says before they came to Blackwater they were homeless rail riders. I try my best to make sure their plates don't stay empty for too long.

The Giant's wife, Legless Fanny, sits up high on a pile of padded cushions and eats cucumber sandwiches and fingerling potatoes as if she is a queen. She bounces along to the upbeat melodies and weeps to the sorrowful ones. Every now and again she warbles out a dainty, falsetto trill.

Percival eats overripe nectarines, mashed bananas, and poached eggs. It doesn't sound a lot like wolf-boy fare, but his double row of teeth makes it difficult to chew. I poach and peel extra carefully for him to make sure he's not in any unnecessary pain. I have learned an entire language from watching the way his facial fur ripples when he is finding something too tough to chew.

Mama Moon loves to tease me about Percival. She knows all about my infatuation, of course. That is the downside of having a psychic medium for a boss. When I try to coax her into telling me the things I *do* want to know about she is extremely tight lipped. "Once I tell you what the future holds, then it is set," she always says. "Keep your options open for yourself. You don't want to be growing old here with us."

All my life I have searched for some kind of sacred sign to let me know what my path in life should be. I have prayed for salvation. I have begged for the love of the Lord. I have looked in churches, temples, and hallowed halls, and I have always come up empty. The first time I saw the freaks I recognized something familiar in them. The first time I heard them sing I knew I was meant for this. Well, not cooking catfish and serving swamp cabbages exactly, but I knew my most direct route to God was through their music.

•

One afternoon, Mama Moon sends me down to the springs to collect pond apples for her special jelly recipe. The bubbling brightness of the springs is a shocking contrast to the still black waters of the swamps. Instead of bony-fingered mangrove trees and haunted cypress, the springs are ringed with wild rice, pond apples, and flowering water hemlock. Dragonfly nymphs dart around my ankles as I approach and, suddenly, I hear a sound so sorrowful it nearly rips my heart from my chest. I drop the pond apples and they scatter around me in the spongy grass.

Percival is singing a song I haven't heard before. It is something mournful and magical and somehow freeing all at once. There is a power in it that rivals anything I've ever heard him perform. The hum of the insects quiets as they strain to hear the intricacies of his melody. I can almost catch little pieces of a story that I know is Percival's own life. I have that familiar feeling, like I am going to be saved. My blood crackles and fizzes and I feel precariously close to the brink of discovery. Then Percival's eyes alight on a rolling pond apple and he looks up to see me standing there.

There is something about being alone in the swamps with a gospel singing wolf-boy that feels terribly intimate and a lot like standing before God. He isn't wearing his customary Sunday finest. In fact, he is naked as far as I can tell, but his pelt makes it seem like he's clothed.

"Abby," he says. It sounds so honey-like falling from his lips that I don't even want to correct him.

"Gabby," I say. I will my legs to remain steady and firm. "I'm so sorry. I didn't mean to interrupt."

Percival smiles, a quick flash of white teeth in the glossy darkness of his face. "Gabby," he says. "Come on in. The water is fine." Dragonflies speckle his pelt with fluttery, iridescent shimmers.

I do as he says, though I am terribly shy about stripping down to my bathing suit in front of him. He ogles my hairless skin and I yearn for some kind of congenital flaw to distract him with.

I blush as he scoops some water into his hands and takes a drink. He is drinking the water that we are sitting in. I imagine our two souls fusing together, swirling down past the double rows of teeth and soothing his magical larynx, revitalizing the ebullient purity of those pipes. I grow dizzy thinking about it and try to focus on something else to distract me.

"What was that song?" I ask, brushing a dragonfly from my nose.

"Something from a long time ago," he says. "It's about a girl named Sparrow Foot. She brought an entire bayou to its knees."

I fight back jealousy. I can hear it now. There are traces of another world in his speech. This is the most Percival has ever talked about his past. We all know that the Giant found Percival wandering the bayou and brought him to Blackwater. Neither says much else about it.

"Why don't you ever sing that song on Sundays? It's so beautiful."

"The Giant doesn't care for it," he says. "It's secular."

The water bubbles around us. Soft, green strips of eel grass tickle my feet. Percival's fur floats along with the ripples and currents, swirling like a mermaid's mane.

"What are you doing here anyway, Gabby? Do you like serving people like us? It seems an odd way to spend your time."

This is my opportunity to gush but I am suddenly tongue-tied. "I like the music," I say lamely. It is more than that. "I love the music. You are the people that make it. It is… the closest I have ever been to salvation."

Percival is quiet for a long while.

"Well, it is easy to mistake music for God," he says. His eyes look tired beneath his thick eyelashes. "But the people here aren't any more pious than anywhere else you might go. We just understand Christian suffering well enough to sing it."

"It is more than that," I insist, but Percival shakes his head.

"Don't go making false prophets out of us. We're just freaks that can sing. You are not like us. You can fit in anywhere you want. Why waste your life in this place?"

I am stung by the coldness in his tone. When he reaches over to kiss me I am unprepared and leap away from his grasp and out of the water. Long strands of Percival's fur cling to my wet skin. I breathe in shallow gasps as he looks at me, calm and unperturbed.

"I'm sorry," he says. "I thought that was what you wanted."

I feel small and inexperienced. The spirit of salvation recedes from me so quickly my head is left spinning. "I have to go," I say. I think I say it. I don't know. I know I leave Percival sitting in the water with sad eyes and fur that billows in the current.

I run the entire way back to Momma Moon's house, stubbing my toes on cypress knees and scraping my arms and legs on reaching branches.

"Gabby," she calls as I clatter through the rickety screen door and run to the tiny alcove where I sleep. I can't bear the thought of her trying to talk to me about what happened.

"Don't say a word!" I yell. She always knows too much.

She pauses in the hallway for a moment before saying, "I need you to come down and start on the mudfish after you've had some a rest." Then, thankfully, she shuffles away.

At dinner that night I keep my eyes down while I serve the food. I'm marrying the condiments together when a furry hand extends into my line of sight. It's holding a spider lily. Something about the combination of beast and flower renders me immobile.

Percival smiles at me, both rows of teeth showing from beneath his combed facial hair. "Sorry, Gabby," he says in a dulcet tone. "I didn't mean to upset you. Sometimes I forget how to behave with outsiders." He looks so penitent I am ashamed for overreacting. I don't know why it upset me so much anyway.

"I'm not an outsider," I say, but my voice is so small I'm not sure he can hear it. I'm left holding the wilting flower as the rest of the freaks look on.

"Is something going on between you and Percy?" Daisy asks, narrowing her eyes. Buttercup kicks her in the ankle.

"Nothing," I say. I accidentally slosh some gravy on Clarence's back, but he doesn't even notice it dripping down his thick hide.

"Gabby," trills Fanny from her soft perch beside the Giant. "More tea over here please!" When I refill her glass she leans over to whisper, "Looks like Percy is enamored."

Beside her the Giant is stern and disapproving. For the first time, he looks at me carefully beneath bushy brows as I clear away his mounds of mudfish bones.

•

Percival and I have been meeting at the springs after his morning classes at the Shape Singing School. Our meetings are chaste, though we watch each other with hungry eyes. He finds my tone-deafness amusing and is impressed with my steadfast determination. Each day he runs me through the scales a few times with a wincing smile that even his shaggy mane cannot hide. The other freaks don't care for us spending so much time together. Percival says it's because insiders and outsiders don't mix much around here.

"I would like to be like you," he tells me one afternoon, looking at my hairless arms.

"But I'm average!" I say. "You channel the almighty. You have Jesus running through your veins and singing through your soul!"

"And I am covered in fur," he says. "My teeth hurt all the time. I am a freak."

"You've been chosen as special," I answer. "I would trade in a heartbeat to have a voice like yours. I skin catfish and alligator every day just to be near it."

"You might choose it," he says. "We have no choice."

Percival has not tried to kiss me again since the first meeting at the springs, so my love has grown back and redoubled. I love him like he is the only pure thing in the entire world. I love him like he is going to lead me to redemption. I know for sure I will finally be saved. Everything will change and I will find a place with these people. I will finally be a part of something sacred.

When Sunday finally rolls around, I wear my nicest dress to serve breakfast in. It is a thin cotton material dotted with faded flowers. When I squint, the flowers resemble spider lilies. A cardinal watches me dress from the windowsill. Everything seems meant to be. Mama Moon raises an eyebrow at my appearance but doesn't comment. I stir the grits. I fry the potatoes. I poach the eggs, humming to myself. I act like a gracious hostess as the freaks start to arrive.

"You look lovely today, dear," Fanny trills, but something is different in her behavior. She seems nervous. She is wearing a hat garnished with strawberries and flowers and waving a fan in front of her face with short, frantic movements. The Giant looks more perturbed than usual. He gives me a dark look as they take their seats.

And this is how it continues. Daisy and Buttercup whisper to each other behind dainty, cupped hands. Clarence and Coriander give me slanted looks. Even Horace the lobster boy is agitated and skittish.

When Percival enters, he is not alone. There is a woman beside him, in a tailored dress, her head bent toward him. They are engaged in some very deep conversation. She is not as pretty as the twins, but she reeks of money and class, and something else. It is an entirely new and foreign scent to Gospel Sunday. It disturbs the usual balance. The rest of the freaks give her wide berth, leaving the seats around the two of them empty.

Percival is dressed to the nines. His suit is crisp and his hair is curled and styled. He reeks of spicy cologne and hair oil. He is wearing a pork pie hat topped with a magnificent, swooping egret plume. He is so engrossed in his conversation with this woman that he barely looks at me. He doesn't notice my dress at all. The Giant has to call for his attention before they can start to sing.

Nothing has changed in his voice. It is as powerful and mellifluous as ever. The well-dressed woman is swooning.

When I ask her what she wants to eat she waves me away. I am so distracted by her presence that I can barely concentrate on being saved. I keep myself busy by scraping fish bones into a pile, and overanticipating the needs of my people. When Fanny asks for more tea, I am standing at her back with the sweating pitcher. When Buttercup and Daisy want coffee, I have it ready, with milk and sugar scooped in each cup the way I know they like it. I am one of them, after all. I'm a freak. Even if my appearance doesn't match up to theirs. I am nothing like this new outsider woman.

In the pocket of my dress I have one of Percival's long hairs tucked away. I caress it as he sings, thinking of our deep soul connection. When the concert is over, I keep it looped around my index finger for comfort.

"Gabrielle, I want you to meet Dr. Evaline," Percival finally says, tugging at my dress as I'm passing by with the iced tea. The whole congregation stops chewing to hear his next words. "She came to see us perform this morning. She came all the way from Boston."

"Pleased to meet you," says Dr. Evaline, looking me up and down, searching for a deformity. She looks from me to Percival, then back to me again, a smile forming on her lips.

I hate her with a ferocity that staggers me. I hate that the rest of the freaks are looking at the two of us and thinking I am more like her than like them. I don't reply to her greeting or take the hand she offers. Instead, I fill her glass until it overflows and then stumble off blindly.

"Deaf and dumb?" I hear her ask Percival, as I run back to the kitchen and wait for him to follow me. He doesn't. For the rest of breakfast he remains deep in conversation with Dr. Evaline. When I emerge from the kitchen, he doesn't look at me again, however, there are eyes all over me as I clear plates and wipe down tables.

The Rapture Café empties out quicker than usual. If the freaks are uncomfortable around regular outsiders, they are downright squeamish when it comes to doctors. Many of the breakfasts are half-eaten. Only the Giant stays until the very end, finishing every last bite, his gaze resting heavily on Percival and the doctor.

Back in my room, I throw my grease-splattered dress into a ruined pile on the floor, then storm back out. I ignore Mama Moon as she tries to intercept me and head out across the swamps for the springs in my nubby, old lavender bathing suit. I practice shape-note singing in my head. I recite the psalms and jump over crawling mudfish. I coax, cajole, and pray to God, but there is no spiritual relief to be found. When I get to the springs Percival is not there. They are empty except for some waving eelgrass and a few dancing dragonflies.

•

Percival isn't at dinner, and the mood is tense among the freaks. If anyone speaks to me, I don't hear it. Dinner passes in a blur. Mama Moon helps me clear the plates before excusing herself to go upstairs and lie down. She is tired from all of the heat. I am still scraping catfish bones and mashed potatoes from the plates when Percival comes into the kitchen behind me. His curls have wilted and his suit is creased and crumpled. The egret plume in his hat has lost its showy frill. I can tell he's come to break my heart.

"Gabby," he says. "I'm here to say goodbye."

I stare at the remains of the food as I scrape each plate into the garbage.

"I figured you would be upset. I haven't told the rest of them yet."

"How can you, Percival?" I don't just mean how can he do this to me, I mean how can he do this to all of us. We depend on him. He is our very route to salvation.

"Dr. Evaline studies people like me," he says. "She will pay me to go with her back to Boston."

I am stunned. The freaks are mistrustful, if not terrified, of scientists and doctors. Historically, the world of medicine has not been kind to them.

Percival takes my hand in his. "She's got ideas for treating me. She's going to remove my extra teeth."

"What if your voice changes?" I ask. How could it not?

He parts his bangs so I can see his eyes better. "It will be worth it."

Worth it? I imagine a new and improved Percival and something gives. It shifts and slides and suddenly Percival looks different to me. The god-like glamour fades and the promise of eternal salvation recoils back into the creeping shadows of the swamps. I look down at my hands, chapped and marred from months of spitting fryer grease and soapy dishwater. I want to shout at him. I feel stupid and childish for having such unwavering faith in a fur-covered messiah.

We say goodbye awkwardly, over the remnants of the freaks' dinners. Tonight, Heaven's mana consisted of cornbread, butterbeans, fried garfish, and candied pond apples.

"Boston's not so far," Percival says. "A bus ride away."

He keeps talking but I can't seem to hear him. I stare at his mouth, a tangle of hair and remnants of mashed banana. I always imagined he was proud of his fur, but now I see how it obscures his mouth. It sticks to his crowded teeth, which jut at odd angles. I heave a couple deep sighs to hold back tears. Percival promises to write, then leaves me to finish cleaning the kitchen.

•

Outside, the swamps are haunted. I spend a few moments by myself humming off-key shape notes to an audience of unimpressed cypress trees. Somewhere an owl hoots and jeers at me. The scent of night jasmine floats in the air, and the sky is a warm soup of sorrow and stars that don't form any constellations. I try not to think about the doctor running her hands over Percy's fur, planning all the different ways she knows to make him a regular man. Trying not to think about it is enough to exhaust me.

"I am not a pilgrim. I am a waitress," I tell Mama Moon as I head off to bed. My feet feel like kayaks and my hair smells like fried mudfish. "I can't stay here, but I don't know where I'll go. Can't you read my future just once?"

Mama Moon takes her bandana out of the freezer and ties it around her forehead. She looks as placid as ever as she hugs me tight. "You'll be fine, Gabby. You just need to learn to find your own way."

I don't find that advice particularly helpful, but I know better than to try to coax a fortune out of her. Mama Moon's word is final. I skip my prayers before climbing into bed and staring at the low sloped wooden beams of the ceiling. June bugs click on the window screen. I recall the song I heard Percival singing that very first day that we met at the springs. He taught it to me during our lessons. A freedom ballad, he called it. It replaces the songs of worship and praise I've become so familiar with. When I fall asleep that night there are no egret plumes or spider lilies that wink across my dreams. Salvation is the last thing on my mind.

ABOUT THE AUTHOR

Kimberly Lojewski is a native Floridian. She has an MA in English from Florida Gulf Coast University and an MFA from University of Massachusetts Amherst's Poets and Writers Program. Her stories have been nominated for three Pushcart Prizes, and have appeared in *PANK, Drunken Boat, Gargoyle*, and elsewhere. Her story "Baba Yaga's House of Forgotten Things" won a 2013 Best of the Net Award. This is her first story collection.

ACKNOWLEDGEMENTS

Thanks to all those who first published, inspired, or helped with earlier versions of these stories.

Jersey Devil Press – About the Hiding of Buried Treasure

Prick of the Spindle – The Church of the Living God and Rescue Home for Divine and Orphaned Children

Drunken Boat – Baba Yaga's House of Forgotten Things

Gargoyle Magazine – Swamp Food at the Rapture Café

Fickle Muses – One for the Crow

Black Lantern Magazine – When the Water Witches Come Dancing for Their Supper

Crack the Spine – How to Get Rid of a Ghost (and Other Lessons from Camp Pispogutt)

Nine – The Decline of a Professional Marionette

A special thanks to the folks at FGCU, Jim Brock, Karen Tolchin, and Tom DeMarchi, for all their support and encouragement.

Another huge thanks to the Poets and Writers Program gang, and most particularly Jeff Parker, for your time, advice, and enthusiasm for these stories.

A big, gigantic thanks to Ryan Rivas and Burrow Press. Florida is lucky to have you, the writing community at large is lucky to have you, and my gratitude is boundless. Thank you so much for the time and energy you put into making this happen.

And the last thanks goes to the big, old world for being weird and wonderful enough to inspire us all in so many different ways.

Subscribe

We thrive on the direct support of enthusiastic readers like you. Your generous support has helped Burrow, since our founding in 2010, provide over 1,000 opportunities for writers to publish and share their work.

Burrow publishes four, carefully selected books each year, offered in an annual subscription package for a mere $60 (which is like $5/month, $0.20/day, or 1 night at the bar). Subscribers are recognized by name in the back of our books, and are inducted into our not-so-secret society: the illiterati.

Glance to your right to view our 2018 line-up. Since you've already (presumably) read *this* book, enter code **WORM25** at checkout to knock 25% off this year's subscriber rate:

BURROWPRESS.COM/SUBSCRIBE

Second Wife
stories by Rita Ciresi
978-1-941681-89-3

Linked fictional snapshots of feminine lust, loss
and estrangement by the Flannery O'Connor
Award-winning author of *Mother Rocket*.

Clean Time: the True Story of
Ronald Reagan Middleton
a novel by Ben Gwin
978-1-941681-70-1

A darkly comic satire of academia, celebrity
worship, and recovery memoirs set in a near-
future America ravaged by addiction.

Worm Fiddling Nocturne in the Key
of a Broken Heart
stories by Kimberly Lojewski
978-1-941681-71-8

Fabulist, folkloric and whimsical stories featuring
an itinerant marionette, a camp counselor
haunted by her dead best friend, and a juvenile
delinquent languishing in a bootcamp run by
authoritarian grandmas… to name a few.

Space Heart
a memoir by Linda Buckmaster
978-1-941681-73-2

The story of growing up in 1960s Space-Coast
Florida with a heart condition and an alcoholic,
rocket engineer father.

the illiterati

Florida isn't known as a bastion of literature. Being one of the few literary publishers in the state, we embrace this misperception with good humor. That's why we refer to our subscribers as "the illiterati," and recognize them each year in our print books and online.

To follow a specific publishing house, just as you might follow a record label, requires a certain level of trust. Trust that you're going to like what we publish, even if our tastes are eclectic and unpredictable. Which they are. And even if our tastes challenge your own. Which they might.

Subscribers support our dual mission of publishing a lasting body of literature and fostering literary community in Florida. If you're an adventurous reader, consider joining our cult—er, cause, and becoming one of us...

One of us! One of us! One of us!

2018 illiterati

Emily Dziuban
John Henry Fleming
Nathan Andrew Deuel
Dina Mack
Abigail Craig
Teresa Carmody

Spencer Rhodes
Stephen Cagnina
Letter & Spears
Matthew Lang
David Rego
Rita Sotolongo

Michael Wheaton

Thomas M. Bunting Projects

Michael Cuglietta

Christie Hill

Alison Townsend

Rick Gwin & Peggy Uzmack

Michael Gualandri

Hunter Choate

Nathan and Heather Holic

Rita Ciresi

Drew Hoffmann

Lauren Salzman

Joanna Hoffmann

Dustin Bowersett

Stacey Matrazzo

pete !

H Blaine Strickland

Karen Price

Leslie Salas

Jessica Penza

Randi Brooks

To a Certain Degree

Yana Keyzerman

Erica McCay

Alexandra Mariano

A.G. Asendorf

Sarah Taitt

Winston Taitt

Lauren Zimmerman

Martha Brenckle

Nikki Fragala Barnes

Michael Barnes

Matthew Broffman

Shaina Anderson

Stuart Buchanan

Shane Hinton

Cindy & Frank Murray

Suzannah Gilman

Anonymous

The Huntress Bird Sanctuary

Allie Marini

Matt Lonam

Naomi Butterfield

Peter Bacopoulos

Ted Greenberg

Gene Albamonte

Erin Hartigan

Sean Ironman

Victoria Elizabeth Webster-Perez

Danielle Kessinger

Susan Lilley

Kim Britt

Janna Benge

Kara Black

Rebecca Evanhoe

Vicki Entreken

Jeff Parker

The Noel Family

Cooper Levey-Baker

Aileen Mulchrone

David James Poissant

J.C. Carnahan

Heather Owens

Stacy L. Barton

Whatever Tees

Nayma Russi

MORE FROM BURROW PRESS

We Can't Help It If We're From Florida
ed. Shane Hinton
978-1-941681-87-9

"As hot and wild and dangerous as our beloved (or is it bedeviled?) state, itself."
–Lauren Groff, *Fates & Furies*

"As weird and funny and beautiful and unnerving as you might expect from some of our state's best writers." –Karen Russell, *Swamplandia!*

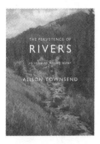

The Persistence of Rivers: an essay on moving water, by Alison Townsend
978-1-941681-83-1

In the vein of Thoreau and Dillard, Townsend considers the impact of rivers at pivotal moments in her life, examining issues of landscape, loss, memory, healing, and the search for home.

Quantum Physics & My Dog Bob
stories by Pat Rushin
978-1-941681-81-7

Each darkly funny story is like a parallel universe where everyday characters find themselves in a reality slightly askew from the one we know.

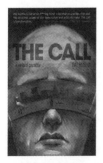

The Call: a virtual parable
by Pat Rushin
978-1-941681-90-9

"Pat Rushin is out of his fucking mind. I like that in a writer; that and his daredevil usage of the semi-colon and asterisk make *The Call* unputdownable."
–Terry Gilliam, director of *The Zero Theorem*

Pinkies: stories
by Shane Hinton
978-1-941681-92-3

"If Kafka got it on with Flannery O' Connor,
Pinkies would be their love child."
– Lidia Yuknavitch, *The Small Backs of Children*

Songs for the Deaf: stories
by John Henry Fleming
978-0-9849538-5-1

"Songs for the Deaf is a joyful, deranged, endlessly
surprising book. Fleming's prose is glorious music;
his rhythms will get into your bloodstream, and his
images will sink into your dreams."
– Karen Russell, *Swamplandia!*

Train Shots: stories
by Vanessa Blakeslee
978-0-9849538-4-4

"*Train Shots* is more than a promising first
collection by a formidably talented writer; it is a
haunting story collection of the first order."
– John Dufresne, *No Regrets, Coyote*

15 Views of Miami
edited by Jaquira Díaz
978-0-9849538-3-7

A loosely linked literary portrait of the Magic
City. Named one of the 7 best books about
Miami by the *Miami New Times.*

Forty Martyrs
by Philip F. Deaver
978-1-941681-94-7

"I could hardly stop reading, from first to last."
– Ann Beattie, *The State We're In*

FORTHCOMING TITLES

Spring 2019

THE GREEN HAND OF VENUS
poems by Susan Lilley

Summer 2019

RADIO DARK
a novel by Shane Hinton

Winter 2019

BRIGHT LIGHTS, MEDIUM-SIZED CITY
a novel by Nathan Holic